FORAGING THE HIDDEN SANCTUARY

THE FORGOTTEN PLANET
BOOK 4

KATE MACLEOD

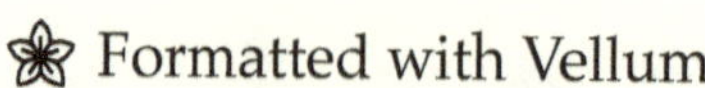 Formatted with Vellum

CHAPTER 1

afayette Eloi had never been able to tune out the wonder of the world around her no matter how hard she tried. Her love of new things just never diminished, no matter what the circumstances. And that was even before her quiet country life had been completely upended.

The pure fact of the matter was, the last few weeks of her life had been incredibly intense and emotionally painful.

First her mother had died from an illness that not even she, the village medicine woman with all her knowledge of herbs and compounds, had been able to cure.

Her mother gone, Lafayette had been pretty

much forced to leave her hometown, the circle of the horizon encompassing just that stretch of grasslands the only place she had ever known. With only her father—who was almost a stranger to her after a lifetime of his long trips away from home—and her late mother's dog Kora—a dog for whom only Lafayette's mother had really existed in the world—as companions.

The dog her father had saved from death by adding robotic components in place of her failing heart and other organs. But those robotic parts just drove a deeper wedge between Lafayette's family and the rest of the village. Remaining there was no longer possible, even if Lafayette had wanted to stay.

Then a few short weeks after leaving her hometown, Lafayette's father had been trapped on a ship as it launched itself into orbit, and it was just Lafayette and Kora desperately trying to make the long journey to the capital city before they ran out of food.

But even the capital city had only offered a brief moment of safety before her foster parent, Uche Okafo, had been taken by the planetary government known as Central Planning. And Lafayette had been forced to watch as all of his books, his life's work as well as her own father's and mother's, burned in a bonfire.

People who were taken by Central Planning were seldom seen again. She thought she knew where Uche was now, but there was no real way of being sure. Not without seeing him with her own eyes.

Collectively, it was all pretty devastating. In her quieter moments, even Lafayette could say that.

But it had also been the most amazing time of her life in a bunch of other ways. She had developed a meaningful bond with what was now truly *her* dog, Kora. And they had formed that tighter bond even before Lafayette had added a computer construct to Kora's robotic body so that the holographic teacher she had found on the ship where her father remained trapped could live on and guide her still. Lafayette had learned so much from that teacher already.

And she had made two insanely devoted friends in Tristan Carey and Dieter Bohm. Although "devoted" felt too small a word to describe two guys who, mere days after meeting her, left with her on a very dangerous mission to find something almost certain not to even still exist under the ice of the north pole, the remains of another crash-landed spaceship.

On top of that, every day they spent together, first on Dieter's family's airship and now on this one they had stolen from Central Planning, was a day she woke up surrounded by an entirely new world. From the plains of wind-swept ice in the north to the growing warmth as they approached the tropics, she was making yet another journey of staggering distance across the curve of the globe of her world. An immense world, still full of things she had never seen before.

It was hard not to be awestruck, even when the risks of their journey edged up higher and higher again.

Like today. She was meant to be on guard for signs of trouble as Tristan climbed the outside of the balloon while their airship was in mid-flight. And part of her *was* really nervous. She knew the dangers as well as Dieter and Tristan himself.

But most of her was still flowing in a state of perpetual wonder. And that was with nothing around them but sea, sky and clouds.

That sky was simply too vivid a shade of indigo, dotted with white clouds near the western horizon, for her not to keep gazing into it. And those clouds had curious shapes to them, as if a fleet of pillowy tall ships was awaiting them there at their destination, another day's travel in that direction.

The water far below them had shifted from the steely blue they had been flying over for the last few days since leaving the polar ice behind to a brighter blue-green color so clear that Lafayette was sure if she just focused long enough past the surface, she could see the bottom of the ocean far below.

But the sun flashing over the crests of waves she couldn't quite see made that kind of staring, if not impossible, at least very inadvisable.

It was all so wonderful, and seeing more and more of the planet she called home was everything she had ever wanted in life.

And yet, the knots in her stomach refused to loosen even a little bit. They took the edge off that wonder. She was incapable of soaking any of it in, even as she felt it washing past her.

"Lafayette?" Kora said softly. As she so often did, she communicated a lot with the few syllables of Lafayette's name. Lafayette looked down at her companion, half orange-furred dog with long swishing tail, half robotic parts that had first kept her alive when old age and grief wanted to carry her away and now housed the more recently added computer construct of a schoolteacher.

"I'm fine," Lafayette assured her. But even she could hear how tightly those words came out.

"I agreed with Dieter," Kora said.

Which was scarcely surprising. Lafayette had been spending more and more time with Tristan, the two of them hard at work recreating as best they could before their memories faded to uselessness all the books that had been burned back in the capital.

Work that Dieter and Kora hadn't really been able to help with. So the dog, naturally, had gravitated to Dieter. Now the two of them were thick as thieves, chatting together in the cant of Dieter's trading family, a language that Kora had picked up much more readily than Lafayette had.

But Kora was still *her* companion; Lafayette knew that. If the time should come when their little foursome had to part ways, she never doubted for a minute that Kora would go with her. There was no reason for feeling jealous, especially since it was her spending more time with Tristan that had started the distance between her and Kora in the first place.

Still. She knew the hurt she had felt had shown on her face when Kora had seconded Dieter's vote. She hated that she had not been as stoic as she had wanted to be. And how awkward it was now, with everyone carrying out the plan with full knowledge that Lafayette was still angry about her role in it.

Or lack of a role.

"I know you did," Lafayette said at last, when the silence had stretched on for so long that even she couldn't bear it. Then she moved away from the dog to peer out the open doorway, careful not to get too close. It was a long drop down to the waters below, and even with her parka on, the air blowing in was cold enough to suck her breath away. They were in the tropics now, sure. But they were still so high in the atmosphere that the air never lost its chill.

"But *you* didn't agree," Kora pressed. "And I've never known you not to be impartial before. It's strange that you didn't see what we all saw."

Lafayette sighed, wishing she could get away from this entire conversation. But the interior of the gondola only had three spaces: where she was now, the cockpit where Dieter manned the controls, and the kitchen which, even if it hadn't been overstuffed with crates, wasn't going to be an escape. Kora would just follow her there.

And she wasn't quite desperate enough to consider jumping out of the gondola door. Although she would really rather be alone just now.

But that wasn't an option.

After a lifetime spent mostly alone, broken up only by the distracted company of her busy mother or, less frequently, the equally distracted company of her busy father, having friends was still a new experience for Lafayette. And she appreciated them; she really did. It was so wonderful to have people around her to eat with, work with, even just to sit quietly with when the mood struck.

But the other side of it was that sometimes you couldn't do exactly what you wanted. Especially not when everyone had gathered around the table after breakfast and made an official vote. A vote you had agreed to abide by the results of before it had been cast.

Lafayette had done her best work painting the signal patterns on the cloth that Dieter had given her to practice on. And she knew she had done well.

But she also knew, as loath as she was to admit it, that her friend Tristan had done just a little bit better. His edges were more defined, his understanding of the subtleties of spacing and thickness of the lines of the code just a little more nuanced.

"His work was better," Lafayette said at last, but very grudgingly.

"It was," Kora agreed.

"But that still doesn't make him the best candidate for this job," Lafayette went on. "Climbing on the outside of the balloon? Tristan is many things —many *fine* things—but being athletic is not one of those things."

"He is wearing the harness and tether," Kora said. "He will be fine."

Lafayette just grunted. She still found it odd that the balloon only had one harness and tether for climbing the system of cables that hugged the sides of the balloon. Given how long they'd been flying without anyplace to land, didn't the designers of this airship give any thought to sudden needs for maintenance? Or did they truly think just one person could handle any problem?

"Hey, you don't think I wish *I* was out there?" Dieter said from where he was leaning against the cockpit door frame, arms crossed. He was in his shirt sleeves, and they were rolled up to his elbows to leave his forearms bare. But Lafayette knew he felt the chill the same as she did. No matter how much they stuffed themselves, he never seemed to add any fat to his lanky frame. And she could see the wind from the open gondola doorway playing through the thick locks of his black hair.

"We need you too much for piloting," Lafayette said at once. "Me, on the other hand…" She ended with a flutter of one hand that she hoped conveyed her general uselessness.

Dieter just scoffed. Which was his go-to response for all sorts of things. Then he turned back to the controls.

"This is taking too long," Lafayette said.

She thought she had said that just to herself,

but Dieter threw back over his shoulder, "It's been ten minutes. Relax."

"You know how meticulous Tristan is," Kora said softly.

"Yeah, I do," Lafayette gave in. She hoped with good grace, but her tonal aim was probably still off. She might've hit closer to sulky.

But she had reasons to be sulky, didn't she? The whole plan was so flimsy.

And yet she hadn't been able to come up with anything better. Especially after Dieter figured out the electronic signaling patterns on the airship's communications equipment. He had switched the patterns they were sending out to every Central Planning airship and ground control station so they were no longer marked as an express ship on a mission of prisoner transfer to the hidden island whose location even on the charts they had found locked in the cockpit had only been marked in faint pencil.

Lafayette had agreed that attempting some sort of con where one of them pretended to be the prisoner in question while the other two pretended to be Central Planning officers was never going to work.

Sure, the ship had all the clearances for that journey. And they had uniforms from the officers they had left on the glacial ice far to the north when the three of them with Kora's help had effectively stolen the airship.

But the clearances were for three prisoners, not one. And not even Dieter, with his bottomless well of confidence, wanted to try bluffing his way through the inevitably onerous bureaucracy of prisoner transfers. The three of them were on those transfer orders, and not for petty crimes. The guards reviewing the paperwork were sure to get wise to what they were attempting.

They were doomed to be found out. There was no way they could get it to work.

So Tristan had come up with this alternative, changing their ship from a prisoner transport to a reconnaissance vessel.

Which, even Lafayette had to admit, was an idea with a lot of merit. For one, that was what the ship had been originally designed for. It had only been changed over for a single mission, and only because it was the fastest airship capable of extended time out over open water. Journeys of that type were not generally undertaken by Central Planning. Or by anyone else, for that matter.

And, as Tristan insisted, the very vague and secretive nature of "reconnaissance missions" would let them answer a lot of questions with a lofty, "That's on a need to know basis." They might not even get any pushback on that one.

All they had to do was change the signal pattern back to the original. The communications equipment would do the bulk of the subterfuge for them. But the security detail at the prison island would do a visual check as well. Through scopes, long before they got close enough to the ground to attempt any other kind of bluffing.

Which meant changing the pattern painted on the balloon's surface itself.

Which further meant someone going out mid-flight to change that pattern with the reflective paints stored in the kitchen. Because while they had seen marine creatures of sizes that boggled the mind, they had yet to see a single island bigger than a steep-sided jutting protrusion of volcanic rock. The kind of rock that was more like glass.

So they had to make the change mid-flight. It was the only way to get close enough to the secret island to land on it. The charts were a little unclear as to the terrain around the prison, but that almost didn't even really matter. If they wanted to see the prison itself, or to catch even a glimpse of any of the prisoners inside, they really needed to set down on the airfield proper, not just anywhere on the island. And without changing the pattern, that was going to involve way too much risk.

Not that this was zero risk either. Far from it.

Lafayette was just glad that none of the bluffing would be on her. She and Kora were too recognizable, and too wanted by Central Planning to hope to escape notice.

Central Planning had sent a fleet of airships to the polar region just to find her. They weren't going to fail to notice her at a prison itself. No way.

But that only irked Lafayette more. Tristan was already taking on all the risk of pretending to be an officer when they reached the prison by mid-morning the next day. So why couldn't she be the one taking the risk now?

She would be much better at scaling the sides of a balloon in flight, she was sure. He was the one who had fallen into a hole barely big enough for him to even pass through. A single hole in a vast field of ice. The sort of feat only Tristan could pull off.

She tried not to remember that that single moment of clumsiness had been what led them to the ship trapped under the ice in the first place. But it was a little unlikely that a second moment of clumsiness was going to lead them to the ship they were after now.

The ship that was definitely in the tropics, but was almost certainly lying deep under all that water.

She still wasn't sure how they were going to undertake such a search from an airship. But pretending to be a reconnaissance airship with clearance to fly wherever they pleased was going to be a start.

Maybe the security station on the island would give them more charts with faint pencil tracings of things no one was supposed to know etched on them.

That would be a rare stroke of luck. But surely they were due one?

As if in answer to that thought, Lafayette heard the unmistakable sound of Tristan crying out. It was faint, but it was as if her ears homed in on it past the constant noise of the wind whistling through the open doorway.

Past the sound of the balloon envelope above her but just out of her line of sight, fluttering at more than the touch of the wind.

Lafayette didn't have a moment to think. She only had time to act. She knew Tristan was falling. She *knew* it.

She lunged toward the open doorway, clutching the frame in one hand and reaching out with the other.

And for a moment she wanted to praise her own luck. She had been just in time to catch hold of his outstretched hand.

But it was no good. He was too far out and moving too fast for her to catch him. She just felt Tristan's cold fingers sliding past hers, their grip not quite connecting.

And then he was gone.

CHAPTER 2

Lafayette bit back a shriek of alarm, leaning further out the doorway in one last desperate attempt to catch him. But he had fallen past her, and the sight of his hazel eyes huge with frightened alarm, even as his falling body shrank in her sight, was burning into her very mind.

She couldn't reach him, but she could catch the line he was trailing behind him.

Before she could quite reach it, a hand closed around her wrist, pulling her in and tucking her arm against her chest so forcefully her twisted elbow flared up in hot protest.

She realized in sudden panic that her booted feet were no longer in contact with the floor of the gondola, but before she could let out the shriek she was still holding back with gritted teeth, she felt herself falling backwards.

Her back was pressed against Dieter's chest, and the arm that had snatched her hand back was still wrapped tightly around her. In one smooth motion, he stepped back out of the open doorway, then sent her spinning away from him and that door and towards the cockpit.

It was like a super aggressive dance move that they had never practiced before. Lafayette's body crashed against the console, but she instinctively retracted all her limbs before she could accidentally knock any of the levers or switches askew as she fought to get her balance back.

Her sense of balance came back in a rush, but it was just a little bit slower than her sense of shame.

What she had almost done had been deeply stupid. If she had caught that line, best-case scenario she would've torn all the skin off the palm of her hand trying to grasp it as it sped past her.

The far more likely worst-case scenario would've ended with her getting jerked out of the gondola entirely. But while Tristan had a harness on that attached snugly around him in a ridiculous number of ways to keep his body tethered to the airship for just this contingency, all Lafayette would have had to save herself from a long fall into the water below would be her grip on the line itself.

A grip surely compromised by the best-case scenario's bloody, rope-burned palm.

She was stupid. Impulsive and stupid.

She didn't even know how to swim.

"Keep it steady," Dieter said. His voice was loud and commanding, carrying over the rush of wind and over the cacophony of her inner monologue both. But his tone wasn't angry or annoyed. It was, in fact, emotionally neutral. But it clearly conveyed a certain amount of cold urgency.

And that splash of cold brought her mind back into focus.

"Right," Lafayette said, reaching for the controls. Not that anything needed any adjustment. Dieter had moved them higher, into calmer air before they had started this little project. The ship needed nothing from her save a bit of attention in case the wind made a sudden change.

Still, she forced herself to keep her eyes focused on the dials and indicators on the console before her, even as her ears listened intently to Dieter's soft grunts behind her. She didn't turn to look, but she could easily picture what he was doing. Hand over doubtlessly gloved hand, pulling up the line that connected the central point of Tristan's harness to the loop in the steel frame just under the gondola doorway.

Tristan wasn't particularly heavy, but he was heavy enough to make this a lot of work for Dieter. Work that Lafayette wouldn't have been able to do at all. Not without the sort of adrenaline surge that had been luring her into trying such a risky rescue in the first place.

Stupid. She would've been pulled right out the doorway. She might've held onto the line past the moment when she'd reached the end of its length with a snap that it was almost like her body could feel right now, when she was just imagining it. But given how long it was taking Dieter just to get Tristan back inside, if he had managed to get them both in at all, it would've taken longer than even she could have held on.

"Lafayette," Kora said, suddenly at her feet. The dog pressed the entire length of her body against the side of Lafayette's shin, like a cat would do. It was meant to be comforting, although being half robot it was less fur and more cold metal with a few knobby bits being rubbed up against her.

But she didn't mind.

"I'm okay," Lafayette assured her. "Just watching what I'm doing here. You know I'm the weakest of the three of us at flying these things."

She heard the sound of Dieter sucking his teeth and stepped away from the controls to let him resume his usual place. He checked everything over twice and tapped one indicator panel with a thumbnail as if he thought the needle inside might be stuck somehow. Lafayette noted that he had indeed slipped on a pair of fingerless gloves, the palms reinforced with an extra layer of thick leather. Just what you'd need to pull in a line without tearing up your hands.

Dieter scowled at the indicator, but then he nodded to himself with a satisfied grunt. Lafayette didn't see how anything had changed, but she couldn't deny that Dieter was a far more experienced pilot than she was.

"Get in the back," he said to Lafayette. Still not yelling. Still not even annoyed, let alone angry. "Tristan is going to need help getting out of that harness. And probably some painkillers as well, from that box on the wall in the kitchen."

"I've got it," Lafayette said.

She stumbled out of the cockpit and saw that the gondola door was once more closed, the wheel spun to the secure position so that not even a whisper of wind whistled through it. In a few minutes she would be too warm for the parka she was still wearing, but not yet.

She ducked into the kitchen and opened the

box on the wall, scanning the neatly arranged contents for the painkillers.

Not bandages. Dieter had only said painkillers. So Tristan wasn't hurt badly. Which was a relief so profound she wanted to stop everything just to sob for a minute. Although that might just be the aftereffects of the adrenaline rush catching up with her.

She made a silent vow to never speak again any of the points she had made before the decision had been reached for Tristan to be the one to go out. She wouldn't point out that his clumsiness had, indeed, been a factor. That she should've been the one to take this risk.

If Dieter wasn't going to bawl her out for her mistake, she just had to follow his lead and show a little more grace too.

But it wasn't easy.

Kora was chatting with Tristan in the back of the gondola, but whatever they were discussing didn't quite reach Lafayette's ears before the two of them heard her coming and let the words fall away.

"You're okay?" Lafayette asked, even as she thrust out her hands, one with a couple of pills on its open palm and the other with a bottle of water she had snatched up on her way out of the kitchen.

"I'm okay," Tristan said. She thought he was trying to smile at her, but what was spread across his freckled face was really more of a grimace. He took the pills and tossed them in his mouth, then uncapped the bottle to follow them up with a long drink of water. He wiped his sleeve across his lips and managed a more convincing smile this time. "There. All better."

"It doesn't work that fast," Lafayette said.

"No, but I know sweet comfort is on its way," he said, fumbling at one of the many buckles on his harness. "Dieter says I won't be really sore until I wake up tomorrow morning, so these pills now and more at bedtime are just to get ahead of it. Although how he knows that, I shiver to think."

"Experience, probably personal experience," Lafayette said. Then she stepped closer to brush his still icy hands away from the buckle. "Let me. Did you lose your gloves?"

"No, they're in my side pocket," Tristan said, standing quietly still so she could get the harness off him. "It was too hard painting with them on."

"Frostbite?" Lafayette asked sharply, grasping his hands to search his fingers for patches going white or gray.

"No, no sign of that," he said. "I was monitoring myself for symptoms as I worked. I was careful."

He flushed as if he realized how that sounded after what had just happened. Lafayette raised an eyebrow, but said nothing.

"I thought this harness was ridiculous when we put it on me, but I think I get the point of it now," Tristan said as Lafayette took a knee to work on the buckles for the straps that hugged his thighs. "That snap at the end of the line was a nightmare, but at least the force of it was distributed all over my body. If we'd just tied a line around my waist, I feel like I would be in two pieces now."

Lafayette just grunted, her attention focused on forcing the stiff leather through the icy metal of the buckles. Her fingers were already aching. But she was scarcely going to complain about that.

Tristan went on. "I should've put my gloves back on before climbing down, though. That was my mistake. Well, that and being in too much of a hurry. But that water is so gorgeous, and Dieter is never going to bring us down any closer to it until we land on that island, is he? It looks so warm, but it feels so cold, you know? Yeah, I was definitely too distracted by the idea of warm sun and tropical islands."

Lafayette felt the sensation of the airship changing elevation, something her body had almost started to tune out whenever it happened.

Dieter was taking them up higher still, further from that water that both Tristan and she longed to see closer.

Although it felt less safe now, somehow, all that water. It was beautiful, and it would lure you in, but it wasn't going to be safe for them, was it? No safer than traveling by air.

Or travel overland, for that matter. Lafayette had encountered far too many ways to die since leaving her home village behind mere weeks before. So many ways to die.

She really needed to learn how to swim.

"Smooth sailing as far as the eye can see," Dieter called back to them. Which normally would sound awfully optimistic from him, but Lafayette knew that statement was really a code.

"I'm on dinner," she said at once, undoing the last of the harness buckles, then leaving Tristan to slip out of the leather straps and stow it with the other airship maintenance gear.

She had dinner to make. And after dinner, there would be another meeting about what was going to happen the next day, when they reached the island. That's what Dieter meant by smooth sailing. It meant now was the time for all of them to gather together, if only for a few minutes, and only with him still in reach of the cockpit controls.

Lafayette already had something of a plan for

dinner, having been the one spending the most time digging inside the crates that were not prepackaged meals, just the ingredients for making meals. She had never cooked on her own until she and Kora had found themselves walking the long route to the capital, and that had been a lot of rice and lentils. Filling, but bland.

But this airship, fully stocked by Central Planning before it had left the capital with its crew of four, gave her so many options.

She got an electric kettle going to soak a package of whisker-thin rice noodles that didn't need cooking so much as gentle warming. Then she whipped up a sauce, whisking together a splash from one bottle or another, and a spoonful from this or that jar, before setting the whole mixture to simmer inside the electric skillet while she hunted down the dehydrated chicken and vegetable cubes that seemed to have changed location since she had seen them last. They only needed a few minutes simmering in that sauce to rehydrate and warm up to something almost as good as fresh would be.

When she was done, she called for the other two, setting their bowls on the crate closest to the door. There was a table in this kitchen, but it was covered in crates of its own, and given that they needed to keep an eye on the cockpit, eating in the doorway had just become their default when they weren't simply eating separately on their own schedules.

"I love the smell already," Tristan said as he leaned his wind-burned face over the steaming bowl of noodles and inhaled deeply. Then he closed his eyes, head tipped to one side in a gesture that was a little too Kora-reminiscent for Lafayette to keep the smile off her face. "Peanut butter for sure," he said, eyes still closed.

"Everything our Lafayette makes for us is very peanut butter forward," Dieter said as he grabbed his own bowl and started shoveling noodles into his mouth without further ado.

"Spicy, spicy, spicy," Tristan said, eyes still closed and food still untouched. He liked to guess all he could by smell before he would indulge in a taste. "Red peppers—dried, I'm sure—but also something else."

"Chili oil," Dieter said around a mouthful of noodles.

"Yes," Tristan said. "But I'm also getting something sweet."

"Honey," Dieter said, still not bothering to swallow first. He nudged Tristan with his elbow. "Just eat already. This smooth wind might not hold out for long."

"Of course," Tristan said, and opened his eyes

to take a careful mouthful of food. Then he held a hand up in front of his mouth as he chewed, unable to wait before saying the words, "Fermented black bean paste, right? I would've had it in a minute, I'm sure."

"Spot on," Lafayette said. Then she finally dug into her own bowl.

She did indeed put peanut butter in everything. But it was so good. And if there was one thing life had taught her so far, it was that good food was something you really missed when you didn't have it. Best to live it up when something as tasty as peanut butter was within your grasp.

"Lafayette," Kora said, not quite plaintively.

"Oh, right," Lafayette said, setting her food aside to squeeze a measure of Kora's nutritive paste into one of the littlest bowls in the kitchen. Being half robot, Kora didn't need much food to maintain herself. But what she did need, she needed on a consistent schedule.

And it was hard to find, the paste that kept Kora alive. Lafayette was still grateful that the amount Dieter's sisters had found for Kora had been ample. It would be months before that would become a worry again. Surely they'd be back in the capital where such things were plentiful before they got anywhere close to running out.

"Right," Dieter said, pushing his empty bowl away and getting up to lean in the doorway, arms crossed as always. "Success, I assume?" he said to Tristan.

Tristan swallowed down what he had in his mouth, looking at the half-full bowl before him with wistful regret, then looked up at Dieter. "Absolutely. As I expected, the original signal pattern design was still visible on the balloon's surface. It was very easy to reverse the changes they had just done a week or so ago. I'm sure it's perfect. Although," he added with a deeper flush to his already red cheeks, "I did drop the paints right at the end there."

"You should secure all gear before changing locations," Dieter said.

"Of course," Tristan said with a nod. But his cheeks were so red now they were shading into violet.

Lafayette had the almost irresistible urge to draw attention away from him before he burst into flames of embarrassment. But the only thing that came to mind was to blurt out, "I *do* realize if I had fallen myself, you would've not had much time to come get me."

"What do you mean?" Dieter asked with a puzzled frown.

"Well, if I were in the water. I'd need you to

come get me pretty fast. Because I don't know how to swim," she ended in something little more than a mumble.

Dieter made a startling sound then, and it took Lafayette a second to realize he had just choked back a laugh that he clearly thought wasn't the appropriate response to what she had just said. Well, she didn't think it was appropriate either. But it *was* confusing.

"Sorry," Dieter said, waving a hand at her growing scowl. "It's just, at this height, whether or not you can swim really isn't an issue."

"You likely wouldn't have survived the fall," Tristan told her glumly.

"But it's water," Lafayette said.

"From this height? It might as well be solid ground," Dieter said. "Which is why… But you know the rest. I don't have to belabor the point."

Lafayette wanted to thank him for not pressing it, but the lump in her throat was making words impossible. So she just nodded. Which somehow just added to the awkward air in the room.

"Right, we have Margo Weiss's uniform," Tristan said, too brightly, but who could blame him for wanting to change the tone? Not that the mention of the name of the girl who Lafayette had once considered a friend, the girl that had been Tristan's own lifelong friend, the girl who had betrayed them all by getting Uche arrested and burning all those books… well, it wasn't the change of tone any of them needed. Still, he pressed on. "It may be too big for you, Lafayette—"

"Even with all the peanut butter you've been eating," Dieter put in.

"—but it fits me perfectly," Tristan went on as if Dieter hadn't said a word at all. "So when we get to the island, I'll be the one doing all the talking."

"Well," Dieter said with a suggestive shrug, not quite gesturing at himself.

"Right, if you need to speak, you already have your character prepared," Tristan said.

"Laconic airship pilot," Dieter said, changing his entire body posture in a flash.

Lafayette had seen him switch from the poor street urchin demeanor that a casual glance would put at maybe twelve years old to the tall, lithe young man that was his true identity before. But this switch was new to her. Now he wasn't just older than twelve; he was older than his actual twenty years. World-weary, ground down by the job. Perhaps a bit unscrupulous, although even she would have to admit that when he tousled up his dark locks all chaotic like that, she always found him a touch nefarious.

"Wait," Tristan said, almost choking on red

pepper flakes before he got his mouthful of noodles down. Then he grinned at Dieter. "You're doing Stewart."

"Oh, yeah," Lafayette said slowly as she finally made the same connection. Slumped and moody like he was now, Dieter looked just like the airship's former pilot. The one who had left Margo Weiss behind on the polar ice despite the fact that the ship was meant to be under her command.

The pilot who had been left on the ice himself along with his two fellow mutineers just a few hours later after Kora had helped Lafayette, Dieter and Tristan overthrow their captors.

"They're going to know you're *not* Stewart though, right?" Tristan said.

"They're going to know you're not Margo," Dieter pointed out.

"I took her name off the uniform," Tristan said.

"And I'm not telling anyone my name is Stewart either," Dieter said. "I'm just conveying his vibes. I doubt anyone is going to be trying to draw me into conversation. I'll be fine."

"And I'll be hiding," Lafayette said, eyeing the empty crate shoved in the corner to the left of the doorway, the corner most likely to be missed by someone doing a visual sweep from the doorway. It was just large enough to hold her with Kora in her arms.

Just.

"It won't be for long," Tristan assured her. "We just need to replenish our stock."

"Of peanut butter," Dieter said.

"But more importantly, we'll be on their systems as out doing reconnaissance," Tristan went on. "They'll ignore us if they've got a label for us. We can search the entire area for the downed ship without ever drawing attention to ourselves. It'll be like we're invisible."

"I know," Lafayette said. She'd be in the crate for an hour, tops. Nothing to panic about there. It wasn't like she was claustrophobic or anything.

She was just a little too used to their plans going sideways. And it was proving impossible to guess what would go wrong ahead of time.

One intense hour where anything could happen, then. After that, they'd be safe.

Just an hour.

But there was no way, even inside her own head, to make the obvious question sound glib and not darkly prophetic.

That question being, what could go wrong?

CHAPTER 3

afayette and Tristan were eating breakfast together in the kitchen, too nervous even for idle chitchat, when they both heard Dieter speaking. Kora, who had been sleeping against the side of Lafayette's foot, lifted her head to listen as well.

Which meant only one thing. He was speaking over the communication system. To the station on the island.

"We're closer than I thought?" Lafayette mused as she scraped the last of her oatmeal onto her spoon.

"Or their range is further out than we thought," Tristan said. "Either way, I guess it's time."

"Time to get in the box," Lafayette sighed. Because Tristan was already wearing Margo's dark red uniform, the sight of which sent a frisson of fear up Lafayette's spine. During their brief interaction with Margo on the polar ice, she had been wearing a black parka, like all the other Central Planning officers. But in her pack inside the airship had been her uniform from the capital.

None of them knew exactly what the different color of her uniform signified. But given how Margo had earned it by betraying all of them and leading Central Planning to a stash of ancient knowledge ripe for destruction in their eyes, it couldn't be anything good.

Lafayette didn't like to think of Tristan as being anything like a member of some kind of secret police. And she didn't like the idea of other people interacting with him under the assumption that's what he was. It sullied him, wearing that color.

But it was one of the key parts of the plan.

"It'll be okay, Lafayette," he told her, reaching across the crate they were using as a table to squeeze her hand. But she doubted he really guessed what she was thinking. He probably thought she was worried about herself.

Or about Kora. Because while the three of them were wanted by Central Planning, they would only be arrested and questioned, and probably eventually stashed away on the very island they were sneaking onto now.

But Kora was to be destroyed, taken apart and studied.

"Time to—" Dieter started to say from the doorway, but Lafayette was already getting up, shoving her breakfast bowl into Tristan's hands before bending to scoop up Kora.

"We're going," Lafayette cut him off to say.

But Dieter didn't seem bothered by the interruption. He just gestured at a smaller crate near the one she was about to crawl into. "I'm going to set that in front of the opening once you're inside. It's empty, so if you need to get out when no one's here to help you, you should be able to shove it out of the way pretty easily. But it will help with making your crate blend in with the others."

Lafayette just nodded, then dropped onto her knees to get inside of the crate.

"No one's going to be checking the kitchen if I can help it," Tristan told her, his cheeks flushing red as they so often did.

"You'll keep us safe, I know it," Lafayette assured him. She settled as far back inside the crate as she could, then helped Kora crawl onto her lap. It was a little awkward, not so much because robotic dog Kora was heavier than living dog Kora had been, because she had hover disks to compensate for that extra weight, but because her robotic abdomen didn't bend. At all. She couldn't curl up like a dog usually could.

But Lafayette found an angle for Kora to sit with her bottom between Lafayette's legs and her top resting on Lafayette's shoulder.

Dieter gave her one last thumbs-up, then swung the side of the crate shut. She heard the sound of the latch closing, a latch she knew from previous practice she could jostle open even from the inside of the crate.

But it still sounded so final, that little click.

Worse was the sound of Tristan's footsteps following Dieter's out of the kitchen. They were both in the cockpit, watching the airship's approach to the island. And she and Kora were alone in the darkness inside the crate.

Then all she could hear was the sound of her own breathing. She was pretty sure it was only her imagination that she could hear the soft whir of Kora's robot parts running.

Kora snuggled her warm nose against Lafayette's shoulder, then settled back into her briefly interrupted nap.

Lafayette was too keyed up to do the same, despite the sleepless night she had spent imagining everything that could go wrong in the next hour. Her heart was hammering at a rate she was sure it couldn't sustain. And yet she suspected it was going to find a way.

She felt the airship descending, mostly by the jostling as they moved through layers of colder or warmer air.

Then she could smell a briny, salty smell. She knew this smell only from books, despite spending days and days flying over the waves. They had only been this close to the ocean water when they were far in the north, and then they had been standing with sheets of fresh water ice separating them from the true ocean water.

But she knew she wasn't wrong. She was smelling the sea.

Then she heard a raucous cacophony of birds as well as another sound, fainter from distance and not quite identifiable. But it was almost like the barking of deep-throated dogs.

She wondered what was making *that* sound.

Then they were on the ground, touching down as gently as ever under Dieter's practiced hand. She felt vibrations that she felt sure were from ground crew catching the lines on the sides of their airship to help make them fast, even though the wind on the ground today was light.

"Going out," Tristan announced, too loudly. He was nominally speaking to Dieter as pilot, but those words were really for Lafayette. To let her know he hadn't forgotten how anxious she must be.

She heard the clang as he opened the hatch, then the sound of his boot heels striking the ground outside. Lafayette scrunched up her face, trying to picture the image that went with the quality of that sound. Hard packed earth? Some sort of pavement like they had in the city? Maybe even stone?

It was hard to tell. But then other steps approached, and someone hailed him before apparently drawing close enough to speak at a normal volume. A volume too low for Lafayette to make out the words. So that left her to obsess over the tones.

Light. Conversational. Not as formal as she would've expected. Which was maybe not a good thing. If the magma-red uniform that Tristan was wearing meant any of the things she was afraid it meant, he should be commanding a lot more respect and less informality.

Which meant whoever he was talking to considered them equals.

That definitely couldn't be good.

Then something else rattled the side of the airship. Refueling, Lafayette guessed after a moment's thought. She could just catch a whiff of something fuel-like, although the ocean smell was still the dominant one. There was also a hint of a dry, dirt kind of smell.

Definitely a hard-packed earth airfield, then.

Her small smile of triumph faded as footsteps strode into the kitchen, but she knew that gait. Dieter. Dieter carrying something heavy. He set it down in the vicinity of the table, then took a spare moment to whisper, "All good. Restocking now, off the ground in under ten."

Lafayette didn't dare answer, and he didn't wait around, anyway. He just headed back out the kitchen door. But he returned so quickly with another crate that she knew someone on the tarmac must be handing things up to him from a stack very close at hand.

He set the second crate on top of the first, but took a moment to fuss with the arrangement as he whispered, "Prisoners in the yard. Only twelve or so, though. No one I know."

Which meant not Uche. But was that good news or bad news?

He came back in with a third crate, setting it near the others and grunting as he stretched his back. "Enough for another two weeks in the air. Good. Good."

Which, she was sure, was also meant to communicate to her that they were nearly done with restocking.

She heard Dieter speaking to someone from the gondola doorway, but too low for her to catch any of it. This was maddening.

It was also getting stuffy inside the box. And she realized that was because the tropics really *were* warm. Warmer than the polar ice cap for sure. But also warmer than even her home in the grasslands south of the capital.

And it wasn't even mid-morning yet. What would it be like here in the afternoon when the sun was high overhead?

Dieter stopped talking, leaving the gondola door open as he headed forward to the cockpit. The airship shook once more, as whatever they had attached to refuel was detached and stowed. They would be airborne soon.

It was working. Their plan was working.

How was that even possible?

Then she heard Tristan burst into the kitchen in an excited furor. Happy excited, not panicked excited, although Lafayette couldn't exactly lay a finger on how she knew that. Still, the temptation to burst out of her crate to see what was going on was strong.

But not until they truly were up in the air. Not until someone came to get her, really. She had no way of being sure of all being clear outside of her crate.

"Lucky thing I'm already packed," Tristan said, but not in a mumble like Dieter had used to communicate with her before.

Then Dieter answered from the doorway, "Take that one too. I'm sure it's all packed as well. You'll need both, right?"

That "right" had a very leading quality to it. One made all the more puzzling by Tristan's hesitation in answering.

"Right," he said at last. "I don't know how… but I'm sure you do. Never mind. I'm off."

"Yes, go," Dieter said. Lafayette had no problem guessing what was behind the tone he used for those words. He very clearly thought Tristan was talking too much.

But what had Tristan's words meant? She didn't know. But her stomach was in knots again.

She listened as Tristan slung first one rucksack and then another over his shoulders. But what two stacks? It sounded like he was taking his own bag—which was a concept panic-inducing enough because why would he do that?—but what could the second bag be? Something that was also all ready to go? Something that Dieter could just point to?

Had they been planning something all along without clueing her in?

No. As confusing as this all was, she knew they would never betray her. Something unexpected had come up, clearly. And they were doing the best they could under rapidly changing circumstances.

She had complete faith in both of them.

But she really wished she wasn't stuck inside a box.

She was just wishing she had brought a bottle of cool, refreshing water inside the crate with her when she felt the airship shudder as the mooring lines were released. Then Dieter was getting them up into the air in a series of controlled bursts. She thought they were pivoting, although to what heading she really didn't have the internal compass to guess.

It felt like it took forever between the moment she was absolutely positive they were at what Dieter called his cruising altitude and the moment when he finally opened the latch and let the side of the crate drop open.

She poked her head out, grateful for the cool air of their current elevation. Then she looked up at Dieter to find him grinning down at her.

"We left Tristan behind," she said, more accusing than she had intended.

"Tristan had an opportunity that was simply not to be passed up," Dieter said, still grinning. But he sobered a bit when she didn't relax her scowl in the slightest. "Even if he had wanted to, it would've blown our cover. He had to take it."

"Had to take what?" Lafayette asked, even as she thrust out a hand for Dieter to help her up and out of the box. But he bent first to fetch Kora, who woke at his slightest touch.

"Oh. The excitement is all over?" Kora asked sleepily.

"No," Dieter said, grinning again. "The excitement is very far from over."

"Because?" Lafayette asked with a sigh.

"Because the reason Tristan isn't here is that he's on a submarine," Dieter said. "And as soon as he can, he's joining us out in open water."

"So we can search above the water and under the water at the same time," Lafayette said, finally feeling like she was a part of things.

Only, she was on the airship with Dieter. Well, that couldn't be helped. Trying to move the crate with her and Kora inside from the airship to wherever this submarine was had probably been too risky.

Although she hoped the idea had at least *occurred* to the other two.

But Dieter was still grinning at her, a grin that

clearly said this excitement was more about her than about him.

"I'm missing something," Lafayette guessed.

"You're missing all your things," Dieter said, giving her one last smirk before heading back to the cockpit. Lafayette swept her gaze around the room and saw that Tristan's bag was missing, just as she had surmised.

But so was hers.

She was, indeed, missing all her things.

"He took my stuff too?" Lafayette asked as she stumbled on legs gone numb from her cramped time inside the crate. But she managed to get to the cockpit and clung to the doorway as Dieter busied himself with this and that on the control panel.

"Well, you're going to need it, right?" Dieter said. "Well, the journals the two of you already filled are still in the back with my stuff. But the ones you're both working on as well as a few spares are in your rucksacks. Who knows what you're going to see and need to record."

"I need my stuff on the submarine?" was all Lafayette could think to say. But saying the words out loud finally clicked everything into place.

She was going to need her stuff on the submarine. Of course. Because Dieter and Tristan already had a plan. And that plan ended with her on the submarine with Tristan.

"They bought our story?" Lafayette asked. She could scarcely believe it.

"Just like we thought," Dieter said. "This balloon is actually delayed arriving at this island because of its polar side trip. But we're a reconnaissance team. We're totally anonymous, aside from being the ones who know the recon passcodes."

"And we had a passcode for a submarine?" Lafayette said.

"Indeed," Dieter said.

Lafayette knew why he was grinning now. And she felt her face matching his, the easiest thing in the world.

But she really hoped they found this lost spaceship in a hurry. Because the recon team they were impersonating were still out there. And they would be heading this way, as fast as they could.

And Margo Weiss, who had commandeered their airship for her personal mission, was still out there too. And something told Lafayette that she, too, was heading their way.

Yes, the faster they found what they were looking for, the better.

But having a submarine was really going to help with that goal.

And Lafayette's grin grew just that little bit bigger at the thought.

CHAPTER 4

Dieter only knew the basics of what had just happened down on the tarmac, but he filled Lafayette in on everything he did know.

Their airship had been expected days ago. That was why the fuel and food restock had been ready to go, just waiting for their arrival. The captain in charge of the guard station hadn't needed to see a thing beyond Tristan's uniform and never asked for any of the documents from the airship cockpit that Dieter and Tristan had so painstakingly modified. It was anybody's guess if even the painting on the outside of the airship had been necessary.

And apparently Tristan had rolled with the mention of the requested submarine, fueled, stocked and ready for departure in the nearby harbor as if he had been expecting such a thing all along. Lafayette could tell that Dieter was impressed with Tristan's acting skills in that moment.

Given that Dieter's entire family were nominally honest traders but secretly black market traders as well as burgeoning revolutionaries, his being impressed was no small feat.

"The captain of the guard pulled Tristan aside the minute he stepped out of the airship, so I only caught snatches of their actual conversation," Dieter told her. "But the ground crew helping me restock the airship was chatty."

"They told you about the submarine?" Lafayette guessed.

"Yeah, but in a different way than Tristan was getting it, I should think," Dieter said. He made a slight adjustment to their heading, scanned the horizon, then glanced back at her again. "There's apparently a small fleet of submarines in the harbor outside the prison. I'm guessing from things they said it's about a dozen, but I didn't dare ask for specifics."

"Right," Lafayette said. She could see how that

would raise suspicions. Better to just let people talk and hope for more nuggets of information like that.

"The submarine they're currently giving Tristan a crash course in navigating is barely seaworthy," Dieter said. "I guess this area is usually pretty placid, which is why it's stationed here now. The other subs are like nothing these guys have ever seen. Very sleek and modern. And numerous. Like I said, there are about a dozen here, but I gather this secret fleet out in the middle of the ocean somewhere numbers in the hundreds."

"And Central Planning has been keeping it all secret?" Lafayette asked.

"Not hard to do when almost no one has ever even seen the ocean," Dieter said.

"And those that have are people like you and your family," Lafayette said. "Seeing it from too far above to notice something like a submarine."

She only knew what submarines were from books herself. But so far books hadn't steered her wrong on very much. Her father's descriptions of spaceships in his journals, for instance, had only been wrong in the sense that they hadn't quite conveyed the actual massive size of them. But given how very large spaceships truly were, it wasn't hard to see why no one reading about them in books could grasp it. Their immensity was almost unimaginable.

Until you saw it for yourself, anyway.

"Barely seaworthy," Lafayette said, circling back to one of his earlier comments.

"Right," Dieter said with a nod of respect for her catching that. "I don't know if you're feeling it too, but—"

"We're on a tight schedule," Lafayette put in.

Dieter barked out a humorless laugh. "Great. We're together on that. We'll likely have to abandon the search because we're fleeing Central Planning closing in on us long before anything happens that could sink a submarine. And I'll always be close by, keeping an eye on things from above. I think it will be fine. They don't cruise as deep underwater as you might think."

"Sure," Lafayette said, all too aware that until he'd mentioned it, she hadn't really had any thoughts on the matter. "So keeping an eye means visual communication?"

"Right. These are not private," Dieter said, brushing his elbow against the communication equipment. "And I wouldn't trust it even for speaking in code. And trying to send encrypted messages like we did from the bridge of the ship under the ice would be a huge red flag."

"But you have a plan," Lafayette guessed.

"Tristan and I have a system for exchanging very rudimentary information visually," Dieter said. "We came up with it when we were kids, but it will adapt to these distances just fine."

"If the submarine is floating on the surface, can't you just land on it? Like we did on the ice?" Lafayette asked. No long-distance communication would be necessary if they could just talk to each other face to face.

But Dieter was already shaking his head.

"I didn't mean with harpoons and winches, obviously," she clarified.

"No, I got that," he said. "But even securing a line and pulling down close enough to hear each other isn't advisable. The waves are too unpre-dictable. Too risky."

"Okay, so that brings me to my real question," Lafayette said.

"Oh, we'll run a line down to the submarine to get you and Kora there, no worries," Dieter said.

Lafayette tried to picture what he could possibly be thinking, but gave it up with a little shake of her head. "How?" she asked at last.

"Kora has her hover disk, so she just needs a tether to you to keep her from drifting too far off target," Dieter said.

"I hate to admit it, but I was really worried about me," Lafayette said.

Dieter just grinned. "I can rig up the harness you wanted so badly to wear before to run along the line like a zip-line. Easy peasy."

"Straight down?" Lafayette asked.

"Well, the least slope I think we can get away with, so not quite straight down. But yeah, steep," he said. "Don't worry. It'll heat up a bit, but it'll be fine. And you only have to do it once."

"I don't like the sound of this at all," Lafayette said.

"Well, you can't stay here," Dieter said with mock sternness. "All your stuff is down there with Tristan."

"And Kora?" Lafayette asked softly. "I'm sure your plan for her is a sound one, but Dieter. Don't you want someone up here with you? For, I don't know, safety?"

Company. She meant company.

But Dieter just shrugged her words off. "Kora belongs with you, right? She's your teacher."

"Dieter—" Lafayette started to object, but he belayed her words with a single raised hand.

"You and Tristan are going to be inside a strange vehicle that he's currently getting only the most minimal of training in," Dieter said. "And it's, as we've already discussed, barely seaworthy. If anything should go wrong, I would rather she was there to help you out than with me, just keeping me company."

Lafayette flinched at how well he could read her mind.

But he wasn't done. "Also, if we find this ship—"

Now it was Lafayette's turn to interrupt. "When we find this ship."

"Yes, when we find this ship," he conceded with a nod, "You'll need her help figuring things out. It might be exactly like the ship we were just on, but it might not be. And being underwater, as it almost certainly is, is going to make any time we spend on it way more complicated."

"And time is short," Lafayette finished for him.

"Yes, time is short," he agreed. She felt him turn his attention back to his flying, his usual non-verbal way of not so much dismissing her as telling her she was free to go.

But there was still one more thing that she had to ask about.

"Twelve prisoners, you said you saw?"

"Twelve exactly," he said. "They were in drab khaki uniforms with shoes that were far too flimsy to escape over the rocks outside the prison walls." He glanced back at her then, making the briefest eye contact. "It's like the other places we've seen, mostly volcanic rock and lots of volcanic glass. It's bigger and flatter, but mostly it's that. I don't think escape attempts are a worry for the guards here."

"No, I don't suppose so," Lafayette said. It was why they moved people here, after all. It was a secret place, only barely spoken of in easily dismissed rumors, and it was surrounded by miles and miles of ocean water.

And, like Lafayette was all too aware, no one in her country lived close to the ocean shore. The mountains east of the capital were too much of a barrier. And there was nothing out past the mountains worth the trouble of going east for.

"Even so, there was a guard for every prisoner while they were shuffling around that dry, dusty yard." Something was catching at his throat, but he was ignoring it, so Lafayette did her best to ignore it too. "I've never seen such broken people in my life. And, Lafayette, I've seen some things. Things I don't want to remember, let alone share."

"I know," she said, giving his shoulder a little squeeze. "I mean, I understand. You don't have to say more."

He just nodded, taking a minute before going on. "Anyway, I didn't see Uche among them. I can say that for sure."

"But the prison is too huge to just be for twelve people, right?" Lafayette asked, really wishing she had seen it for herself.

"Everything there felt half abandoned," Dieter said. "Rundown and old, and the guys I was chatting with in the ground crew had a feeling about them. Like this was where you get assigned when all your other assignments don't exactly go well."

"But there's a shiny new fleet of submarines," Lafayette said.

"Yes, there was definitely a feeling like sudden, unwelcome change was on the horizon," Dieter said. "The screwups of Central Planning are about to find out that even here in the middle of nowhere, they're still part of Central Planning. I predict some friction. Hopefully after we're gone."

"Uche might be there," Lafayette said.

"Or he might not be," Dieter said. "He might still be in the capital, where my brothers are looking for him."

A gentle reminder, but one she knew she had needed.

Still. "I'd hate to be this close to him and only find out later that I could've done something to get him free," she said.

"Well, I'd hate to see you try and then get caught yourself for your efforts," Dieter said. "Whether he's there or not, but particularly so if he's not. Which we don't know if he is or isn't."

"If only we had a spy on the inside," Lafayette sighed.

"Let's just focus on finding this missing spaceship," Dieter said. "I think that's more than enough on all three of our plates."

"Four," Kora put in from where she was sitting, leaning against Dieter's leg as he piloted the airship.

But Dieter didn't answer. He just made another little adjustment to their heading.

Lafayette tried to make herself useful. But with all of her things inside a submarine somewhere far below her, she couldn't work on her journals. And after making lunch for Dieter and herself, there wasn't much more she could do. So she just perched in the back of the airship where she wouldn't be a hovering distraction for Dieter and kept her eyes on the water below.

But if she was hoping to catch the outline of a sunken spaceship, she was bound to be disappointed. Although she did at some point work out that Dieter was flying them in a slow, lazy circle. A circle so immense that they had only made two revolutions before the sun finally touched the horizon to the west.

Only then did Lafayette see a glint in the waves below. Just a brief flash, but it drew her attention to one specific part of the wide expanse of waves below the airship.

Then it flashed again, the light from the setting

sun reflecting off something. But no submarine could possibly be that shiny. No, she was sure what she was catching was the reflection off a mirror.

"Harness time!" Dieter yelled back from the cockpit, as much as telling her that he had seen the glint too.

"Got it!" Lafayette said, and pulled out the harness that had saved Tristan's life just the day before. She made quick work of the buckles, then checked them all a second time before Dieter came out of the cockpit to open the gondola door.

Lafayette braced herself for a blast of cold air, but while she had been strapping in, Dieter had been bringing the airship down as low as he dared. Far lower than they had been since leaving the ice cap, save for their moments on the airfield on the island. Consequently, the air that slapped at her face was warm and filled with salty spray.

The smell was divine. And the warmth was like a full-body hug.

"Line is good to go," Dieter said, motioning for him to join her at the doorway. While Lafayette had been gazing out the windows, Dieter had been both flying the airship and constructing a harness remarkably similar to the one Lafayette was already wearing, this one for Kora. It had a single line clipped to a loop on her back between her shoulder blades, and he was holding the clasp at the other end, waiting for Lafayette to be within his reach. Once she was he turned her halfway around to clip Kora's line to the back of her harness.

"Just to keep her close," he reminded her, and she nodded, suddenly too nervous to speak. Then he was clipping another line to the front of her harness, just where Tristan had been clipped the day before.

"See you in a few days," he said with the kind of grin that instantly put her on high alert.

For all the good that did her. He clapped her on the shoulder, she thought in a goodbye kind of gesture, except he kept pushing on that shoulder, shoving her towards the door. Then his other hand found the middle of her back and thrust her outside the gondola, and she was falling.

Her panic was in no way lessened when Kora gave a hoot of delight before leaping out after her. Sure, she had hover disks. She could control the rate of her fall if she wanted to. Lafayette suddenly had so many more questions about this process that she really wished she had asked Dieter before he'd pushed her out of his airship.

She was terrified that she might get a limb tangled up in that line, or might accidentally close her hand over it and burn her palm. The best she could do was pinwheel her arms and try to tune out Kora's continuing shrieks of joy.

Apparently, this was fun for the dog.

But something changed about the angle of the line. Dieter must be moving the airship even lower, leaving enough slack in the line to slow her descent.

Then she was colliding with Tristan's body with a shared "oof" between them. Tristan's hands on her shoulders made sure she was steady before he bent and released the line that ran from the airship above to an anchor point by the open hatch of the submarine.

The submarine. She was here. She was finally down among the waves. She could feel the spray as they hit the sides of the submarine.

Rocking the submarine rather violently, frankly.

"Come on," Tristan said, stepping back to the far side of the hatch without letting go of her shoulders. She saw he had a tether of his own, a short one clipped to the same anchor point as she had been.

As she was no longer. And Kora's only anchor point was *her*.

"Climb down first," Tristan said. "I'll follow. I want to get this hatch closed before one of these waves swamps us."

Lafayette couldn't argue with that. She fumbled around until she found the top steps of a metal ladder leading down into the darkness of the submarine's interior.

And now she was *under* the waves. Another day, another entirely new world to see.

CHAPTER 5

t took a moment for Lafayette's eyes to adjust to the relative darkness of the submarine's interior. Which, given that it wasn't quite roomy enough inside to stand up in even for her petite height, was a bit of a problem. She smacked her head twice on two separate metallic things she couldn't quite see before she let Tristan's hands on her shoulders guide her down to kneel on the floor of the space.

The floor was cold metal covered with a thoroughly inadequate layer of rubber matting. The matting was worn through in patches, one of which was directly under Lafayette's knee. She could feel the metallic chill even through the cloth of her pants, but once she shifted herself so that both knees were resting on the mat, it wasn't so bad. It was still hard enough to hurt her joints if she put too much weight on them, but at least the rubber kept the cold at bay.

"I thought this was the tropics?" Lafayette said, reaching out for Kora as she used her hover disks to levitate down inside the submarine. Kora settled against Lafayette's side, although Lafayette doubted very much that the dog's computer-enhanced eyes were having as much trouble picking out details in the world around them as Lafayette's were.

She could see they were in an almond-shaped space, tapered in the front and in the back, although the walls themselves were covered with an elaborate network of metal pipes and plastic conduits for electronic wires to pass through.

She was just squinting at the front of the vessel, where the controls were arranged around a slightly thicker pad of matting that must function like a chair for the pilot. But just when she was starting to make out the individual control levers and wonder at their functions, Tristan shut the hatch and thrust the entire submarine into almost total darkness.

"No lights?" Lafayette asked, trying to laugh

off her fear. The resulting nervous twitter wasn't really coming off as nonchalant.

"There are," Tristan said in a hedging tone. Then he brushed past her, hands over his head touching the pipes that ran above in a motion that was probably meant to keep him from braining himself like Lafayette had just done.

Then he settled onto the thicker padding in front of the controls, legs crossed in front of him. The seat only lifted him about ten centimeters off the rubber mat that Lafayette was sitting on, and the controls were crowded around him on all sides so snugly he really didn't have much choice but to cross his legs.

Then he looked back at her, and even in the darkness his smile shone bright. "There are interior lights, but I prefer the exterior ones."

Then he threw a switch, and Lafayette's breath caught. She had known they were underwater, but now she really *knew* it. She could see long fronds of seaweed waving just in front of them, tiny fish darting in and around the bubble-speckled surface of those waxy green leaves. The last of the light from the setting sun was gone now, and neither of the moons had yet risen, so the water past the reach of their lights was all murky darkness. But in front of them it was a rich, dark blue so vivid it was like they were immersed in an ocean of paint.

"I wish Dieter could see this," Kora said wistfully.

"I just wish he wasn't alone up there," Lafayette said. "I don't think it's safe."

"He's going to find a place to put the balloon down at night," Tristan said confidently.

"I don't know," Lafayette said. "We haven't seen anything but sparse rocks until we got to the prison island. And landing anywhere like that would really be pushing our luck."

"It's an option in emergencies," Tristan said. But he was digging in a flat leather pouch that was affixed to the side of the submarine, perfectly located to be within his reach from the seat at the controls without being in his way when he was piloting. He pulled out a heavy stack of paper, bound with brass fasteners but with no proper cover to keep the pages from curling from use. He handed it back over his shoulder to Lafayette.

Lafayette leaned in close to squint at the top page, but Kora leaned in as well, firing up her green indicator lights to their brightest setting. Green wasn't ideal for reading light, but it worked well enough for Lafayette to realize that what Tristan had handed her was a stack of nautical maps.

"There are islands," she said. "Lots of them."

"Mostly south and east from there, but yes," Tristan agreed. "I'm going to take us closer to the one that's circled on the second page. It has a nice harbor that will protect us from the tides and currents moving us about long enough for us to get dinner and some sleep. It might even be possible to go ashore from there. We'll see. But in either event, we can start making search sweeps for the sunken ship in the morning."

"I don't suppose the fellows who loaded up this submarine with supplies for you had any rumors to share about sunken spaceships?" Lafayette asked as she turned the pages, studying each map in turn. They were so detailed, but most of the labels were written in a sort of… well, probably not a code. She got more the sense that this was not just technical vocabulary but one that used a lot of shorthand and abbreviations that she just didn't know. But it wasn't someone deliberately trying to hide information, it just assumed she had more background knowledge than she had.

Although she was pretty sure that meant it was going to be harder to work out what it all meant than if it *had* been words she already knew but in code. But Kora with her teacher construct knew all sorts of things. The two of them together would work it out.

"The islands are south and east, but the deeper waters are north and west," Tristan said. "What we're looking for, it's far more likely to be in deep water than shallow."

"Unless it broke up a lot on impact," Lafayette mused. "But neither of the other two ships were damaged much at all. One we know for a fact was still flyable, since it launched itself into orbit. The second I know we could've taken up into space ourselves if we had tried. Do you think hitting water would make damage more likely or less?"

"I want to say less, but I don't really know," Tristan admitted. "Also, there's what's left of the ship in the capital city. That one wasn't flyable."

"Yes, but I don't think that was because of crash damage," Lafayette said. "I think the first settlers scavenged it for parts until there was nothing left but the bit jutting up in the center of the city."

The bit that was there in plain sight, but no one seemed to notice it. It looked like a tower, but nowhere else on the planet had a tower remotely like it. It was so tall, and the top was covered with a miniature city of its own where Central Planning had all of its administration buildings. She hadn't been up there. She'd only gone a short ways up the shaft part of the spaceship. But she had gotten glimpses of the surface structure from the ground.

She would've never guessed it was a spaceship either. Not until she'd been inside it.

"We have sharper eyes now," Tristan told her. "I hope we find something intact like the one you and your father found south of the grasslands, or like we all found under the ice up north. But even if what's left is broken up and covered with later construction of some kind, we know what to look for now. We'll spot it."

"It will certainly help that no one has built any-thing out here but that prison," Lafayette said.

"Well, so far," Tristan said. "The buildup of their submarine fleet isn't exactly an isolated event. There are plans to shift the island facility from a prison to a military outpost. Why, I have no idea. Who's the enemy way out here?" He shrugged, then shook his head in frustration.

"If it's no longer going to be a prison, what are they planning to do with the prisoners?" Lafayette wondered.

"I did ask that," Tristan said, even as he leaned forward to release some sort of anchoring mechanism. Lafayette felt them floating free, bob-bing with the tide for a moment before Tristan goosed the engines and guided the nose along a course out of the forest of kelp and into deeper waters. The blue was more intense here, but also darker.

"And?" Lafayette prompted after Tristan had finished guiding the submarine in an arcing turn, leaving the kelp behind but turning away from the deeper water as well. Now they were skimming along over the sandy bottom. The sand was in humping ridges, dotted with fragments of the now-familiar volcanic rock. Those fragments clearly housed living things, although Lafayette never quite caught more than a glimpse of them as they scurried out of sight the minute the light touched them.

"There are fewer than four dozen prisoners there now, in groups of twelve that never mix with each other," Tristan said. "I only saw the same twelve that Dieter saw. I assume he already told you that Uche wasn't with them."

"He did," Lafayette said. "But he didn't know about the other three groups."

"Yeah, but still," Tristan said. "That's not a lot of people. Not compared to the number of people I *know* have disappeared from the capital just in the last year. They don't keep many people here. So I suppose the ones here might just go to wherever all those other people are."

"But?" Lafayette said. Because she could hear

the hesitancy in his voice at accepting his own supposition.

"Well, I didn't get the sense that the guards thought that was going to happen," he said. "Their words had too much of an air of finality to them. Like all they were going to do before going was… how did he put it? Clean up."

"That sounds bad," Lafayette said, and found herself hugging Kora tightly.

"We'll find this ship and figure out how to use it to get to your father," Tristan said. "Then we'll use it to get to Uche, too. There's got to be a way we can do that, right? It's something so far beyond anything that Central Planning has, it just has to give us a tactical advantage."

"Assuming it's even still there," Lafayette said.

"We saw its signal from the polar ship," Tristan reminded her with a firm set to his jaw. "We know it's there. And intact enough to appear on the other ship's sensors. It's there."

Then he turned the nose of the submarine once more, guiding them in bursts through a narrow gap between two immense ridges of volcanic rock. There was barely enough room for even their tiny submarine to squeak by, but the water was calm and Tristan's hand on the controls was sure.

Beyond the gap in the rock, they reached a wide, sandy-bottomed pool that was just barely deep enough to keep them from running aground. Tristan pivoted the submarine around until they were facing the direction they had just come from, then threw a pair of levers on either side of him. Lafayette heard a rattle like chains and then a pair of soft thunks.

"We're anchored," Tristan said, reaching his hands up high over his head and arching his back. "I can teach you how to pilot this thing tomorrow so we can take shifts like on the airship. But for now, I'm beat. Let's eat and sleep."

"Sure," Lafayette said, twisting around to look towards the back of the craft. There was a modest stack of crates there, but nothing like a kitchen. Or any kind of separate room at all.

"Some things are going to be a tiny bit awkward," Tristan said with an apologetic wince. "It's close quarters, just this one space. But there are enough food rations for both of us for at least two weeks, preserved food meant to be eaten as is, no cooking required. And two bedrolls. I assume you and Kora can share."

"Yeah," Lafayette said.

"The tank on the wall back there is the desalinator," Tristan said, pointing. "That pulls the salt out of the seawater around us so we can drink what's left. It doesn't taste great, but it didn't make me sick or anything."

Lafayette dug through the crate of preserved meals. They were reminiscent of what her father had packed for their first journey when she'd left her hometown weeks before. But while those meals had required hot water to reconstitute into soups and stews, these meals were ready to eat.

Which was odd, but not unpalatable. What they lacked in spice they made up for in salt, but not quite enough to be off-putting. The vegetable goo had almost no texture and tasted… well, green. But the thick crackers and brightly orange spreadable cheese were actually quite addictive.

If only they had peanut butter in there as well. But, alas, every pack Lafayette scanned the labels of as she ate her goo all listed cheese with the crackers and never peanut butter.

She hoped Dieter appreciated it, alone on the airship with all the peanut butter.

Then Tristan opened a different package and pulled out a rectangular baked pastry. He broke it in half, sending scatterings of crumbs and bits of sugar all over the rubber mat between them. But when Lafayette took a bite of her half, she almost hummed aloud with pleasure.

"Apple pie," Tristan said, sharing her smile of delight. "I don't even mind that it isn't warm."

"Me neither," Lafayette agreed.

Then Tristan took the charts that Lafayette had

set aside and started turning through the pages, and the two of them planned their first search grid as they ate sweet, cold baked apples laced with cinnamon.

And Lafayette simultaneously hoped they found what they were looking for soon, and that this time with Tristan exploring the ocean and eating cold apple pie together would never end.

CHAPTER 6

The days fell into a comfortable rhythm. They woke each day in the same cove and ate a cold breakfast of oatmeal that had been baked into bars studded with bits of dried fruit and nuts, which were surprisingly filling.

Then they'd check the charts they had marked up the night before, and one or the other of them would take the controls, guiding them out of the cove and towards the deeper blue waters.

Lafayette was a little sad that they started their days so early and ended them so late that she never saw the cove's sandy beach by sunlight, or even saw much of the sun filtering down past the waves. By necessity, their search grids took them deeper and deeper each day, further and further away from the sunlight.

But if her life had become a perpetual night-time, it was a terrifically interesting one. Tristan had figured out how to angle the lights up from the sandy bottom of the ocean, out to the far distance. This made the light bright enough to guide their way and avoid unexpected obstacles, but not so intense that the aquatic creatures fled before they could be properly seen.

Especially when the currents were carrying them along and they could cut the engines for a time, they caught glimpses of all sorts of things. Whichever one of them wasn't piloting was on sketching duty, trying to take it all down before it was gone from sight. The variety of creatures was mind-boggling. Just the various designs of their fins and tentacles that they used to propel themselves, Lafayette could easily see devoting an entire book just to studying the details of that.

The interior of the submarine started to feel a bit gritty. They tried to be careful with crumbs, but soon there was also sand in that mix. Because after the first day spent under the waves, they had agreed they needed a break from the tight space. They had stripped down to shorts and sleeveless tops and made their way through the day-warmed water to the sandy beach of the cove.

Moving through the water wasn't as frightening as Lafayette had assumed it would be. Not that she could call anything she was doing swimming. But Tristan knew how to keep his head above water, and he showed her how to kick her feet to match him. He still stayed close by her side, ready to grab her arm and pull her up if she should start slipping down under the waves. She appreciated that.

But she really appreciated the little break going ashore gave her to find just a little privacy off in the ferny undergrowth. They were both conscientious about ignoring what either of them had to do in the back of the sub, but still. Real privacy was always preferable.

Then, on the third night, Dieter unexpectedly joined them. He had found an open glade amongst the palm trees, just large enough for him to set the airship down. At the sound of his voice, Kora emerged from where she had been napping in the submarine and floated ashore using her hover disks to keep her above the water. She never even got her paws wet. And after that, they all started eating dinner together on the beach each night and planning the next day's search grids together.

Dieter, from his position in the sky, couldn't see much below the waves, although he was certain if there were a spaceship down there, he'd see the outline of it unless it was very deep indeed. But mostly his role was as lookout.

There was some sort of diving suit that was stowed on the submarine's exterior, but when they all swam out to look at it, it didn't seem viable as a way to send one of them out separately to expand their search. It had no way of moving on its own save bouncing around the bottom or very laborious swimming, and it was far too heavy to allow any of them to get much speed.

Also, it had no independent source of air. It was meant to always be attached to the submarine by a series of hoses. They quickly abandoned the idea of one of them using it and got back to work planning searching grids with just the submarine and airship.

They all agreed at some point their ruse was bound to be uncovered. They had left Margo Weiss and her crew on the glacial ice, but they had known at the time that the crew as well as Margo would be rescued within a few hours. They had, in fact, counted on it. As much as Margo had betrayed them, and her crew hadn't been stellar human beings either, Lafayette, Tristan and Dieter didn't have it in them to leave someone to starve or freeze to death on arctic ice.

But once they'd been picked up, they would

surely have gotten back to work. What that meant for Stewart and his two crewmates, the three of them couldn't really guess. But there was no question that all Margo would do was direct her energies at getting the three of them plus Kora back in her power again. Keeping her rank and privilege depended on it.

So Lafayette and Tristan scanned the bottom of the ocean for the remains of a starship while Dieter scanned the skies for trouble.

At least the weather was holding out.

And, small and gritty-floored as it was, the submarine remained a comfortably cozy space where Lafayette and Tristan spent the entire day and almost the entire night practically on top of each other. They shared meals, swapped piloting and sketching duties, and chatted together with warm camaraderie. And after swimming back from the beach each night, they'd dry off, then spread their bedrolls out in a space barely large enough to even hold them both. Then they'd lie together, chatting softly as Kora snored by Lafayette's feet.

But soon their supplies started to dwindle once more. Fuel more than food, but that almost made it worse. Lafayette knew from practice that they could ration themselves and get by with less food to press through a search. But it was impossible to ration fuel on an airship or a submarine the same way.

"We need to go deeper," Tristan said. "That darker patch we keep circling around, the one where the sandy bottom ends at a stony drop-off."

"I know," Lafayette said. They had both been avoiding going out that far into the blue without quite discussing why. Lafayette wanted to say it was because there was no marine life out there for sketching, but she knew that wasn't really why.

It was scary, that dark impenetrable blue. And it was scarier still, not being able to see anything below them but more and more blue that faded all too quickly into black. It was unnerving, when one or the other of them would nose-down the submarine to look, seeing never-ending nothingness below them.

But they had covered all the shallows in the area. As inexact as their assessment of where the dot on the spaceship sensors had been located, it wasn't so far off as all that. It had to be within the search grid they had been covering these past seven days.

And only that dark depth remained.

"It's too small to be a crater, though, right?" Tristan said as he turned the submarine towards the drop-off. "It's so much smaller than the crater we found covered in ice."

"It is," Lafayette agreed. "And it's smaller than the first one I saw, at the southwestern edge of the grasslands. That one was filled with an entire jungle, you know. But this sinkhole in the ocean is much smaller. And kind of oval. Which doesn't seem right for a crater."

"No, with all the volcanic activity around here —dormant now but still—I think it'd have to be what's left from some long ago geological event," Tristan said.

They both glanced back at Kora napping behind them, but she was snoring too loudly to hear the two of them. Which was just as well. The sort of dancing around a topic they didn't quite grasp thing they were doing was just the sort of thing that would bring the teacher out in her.

Not that she had a particularly strong background in geology. She was the first to admit that the construct inside her that had once been a woman named Sameera Adel had been a teacher of young children. The more involved science topics had been the domain of the other two teachers on the spaceship. But even so, she would be prompting them both to think harder about what they already knew if she were awake.

And honestly, Lafayette didn't think boning up on geology was going to help her find this ship.

"You know, the ships when they came down

weren't crashing in the proper sense of the term," Lafayette pointed out.

"They still left massive craters," Tristan pointed out.

"But maybe they didn't have to," Lafayette said. "Or maybe, since this place is water, it made a crater in the water and then just set down on the rock, or made a little damage but not as much as the others. I don't know. But I think it's pretty likely they didn't all come down the same way, and one of the two we haven't found yet could just be parked, ready to go back up into space."

"Launching from the bottom of the ocean might be a bit of a trick," Tristan said.

"We were going to try it to get out of the ice, remember?" Lafayette said.

"Yeah, but we didn't," Tristan countered. "We were only talking about it because we didn't have a lot of options."

"None of this matters until we find the ship," Kora said from behind them. Her nose was still under her paw and her eyes were closed, but clearly she was listening to them all the same.

Then they fell silent, Lafayette and Tristan both leaning forward ever so slightly to watch the last of the sandy ocean bottom pass away beneath them. For a single breath, there was nothing below them but jagged rock, the sand all gone.

And in the next breath, there was nothing below them but darkness.

Tristan adjusted the lights, but no direction revealed anything but murk. It was scarcely even blue any longer, just a midnight color flecked with bits of dust that reflected the light from their submarine like faint stars.

Well, it couldn't really be dust, could it? Maybe it was something like pollen for the aquatic plants. Or larvae or eggs or very small creatures. Without a way to scoop some of it out and look at it under magnification, there was no way for Lafayette to be sure.

"Is there a limit?" Lafayette asked, and realized too late that she was whispering. And yet, speaking out loud in this strange, dark space felt wrong somehow. "Is there a limit to how deep we can go?"

"I don't know," Tristan admitted. "I get the sense these things aren't usually used for going this deep. They're for spying on other people, right? You don't have to go all the way down here to do that."

"All the water above us," Lafayette murmured. "That's a lot of pressure."

"There is a gauge here," Tristan said, hitting it with his thumbnail in a way that was entirely too reminiscent of something Dieter would do.

"It measures stress on the hull. It says we're fine."

Lafayette nodded, but she wasn't sure if she wanted to trust that gauge. She had never seen the needle inside it move at all. Maybe it was broken.

"We do have an oxygen limit," Tristan reminded her. "We go up at sunset every night to eat and sleep, but the fact of the matter is we don't have enough air to stay down much longer than that. We have to get topside and open the hatch or we'll asphyxiate."

"Good to know," Lafayette said, suddenly feeling a little short of breath. Which was completely ridiculous. It wasn't even lunchtime yet.

"The canyon on the charts goes in this direction, so I'm going to angle us so we're following it," Tristan said, making some adjustments to their heading. "I'm sure we'll see rocks ahead of us in plenty of time to compensate, but still. Our best odds of finding anything are striking down the middle, right?"

Lafayette was starting to doubt even their best odds were going to be good enough. It was just so dark down here, and their lights penetrated such a little part of it directly ahead of them. It would take a huge stroke of luck to find anything in those circumstances.

But she had forgotten to take one thing into account.

What they were looking for? It was truly huge.

And in the middle of the afternoon, that fact was really brought home for her. Because there was no mistaking the gentle curve of darkness that was darker than the other darkness when it loomed up ahead of them. It was so large that it felt like they slowed down approaching it. It should be getting bigger faster, but it was so big that it was actually much further away than it looked.

"That's it," Tristan said, his excitement making his voice jitter and jump. "That has to be it. What else could look like that?"

Lafayette didn't answer. She just leaned in closer, nearly pressing her face against the cold glass that was all that separated them from all that water.

Then she felt Kora's body squirming into the narrow gap between her side and the wall of the submarine. She tried to make a little room so the dog could see too, but there wasn't a lot of room to play with.

The three of them were silent as they chugged closer and closer to the increasingly defined out-line of the ship. It had a faint glow to it, not from any particular light source, more like the ship itself was emitting a low frequency of light.

"Shields are up?" Tristan pondered.

But Kora made a low sound in her throat. Not exactly disagreeing, but more like something was bothering her.

"What is it?" Lafayette asked her.

"It doesn't look quite right," Kora said after a long moment's thought.

"What do you mean?" Lafayette asked. "There's the wheel above us now, and its nose is down that way, maybe wedged into some rocks or another sandy bottom or something."

"No, she's right," Tristan said. "It's not the same as the others." Then he flushed a little before adding, "I know I didn't see the first one, but you described it and I saw your drawings as well as your father's."

Back before Margo had burned them all.

But Tristan wasn't done. "It's a spaceship, no doubt about it. But look at the details. The way the wheel meets the shaft. That's an entirely different spoke system."

"You're right," Lafayette said, seeing it at once now that he had pointed it out. "And the main part is much clunkier than the other three ships. Not so sleek."

"It's an older design," Kora said. "I'm sure of it. In fact, I know what this is."

"What is it?" Lafayette and Tristan asked as one.

"It is, it has to be," Kora said, but clearly just to herself. Like she didn't quite believe the conclusion she had already come to.

"What is it?" Lafayette asked again.

"It has to be," Kora said again. "It's the remains of the first scout ship. The one that reached this planet centuries before the fleet I—I mean, Sameera Adel—was on. This was the ship that reported back that the planet was habitable but uninhabited. Suitable for settlement. This was the ship that called the rest of us to follow after it."

"Before it mysteriously disappeared," Tristan guessed.

"Yes," Kora said. "We came after we got its preliminary report, but we never received any of the secondary reports we should've been getting. We didn't know what had happened to it. I guess no one in the fleet ever found it."

"Not until us," Lafayette said. "Generations upon generations later."

"We found it," Tristan said.

"It's not the ship we were looking for," Lafayette sighed.

"Yeah," Tristan admitted. But he was grinning at her again. "But that doesn't mean we aren't going to find a way to explore it while we're down here, does it?"

CHAPTER 7

Tristan and Lafayette spent so much time guiding the submarine around the spaceship as close to its hull as they dared that they couldn't even start making their way back to the cove before they had to surface and open the hatch to get a breath of fresh air. But opening that hatch far from the safety of the harbor brought in more than air.

Lafayette couldn't help shrieking when the first wave broke past Tristan's body as he held the hatch open, splashing over her toes and running all over the already dirty floor of their submarine.

"That was a big one," Tristan said with a nervous laugh. "It's not too choppy here. We'll be fine.

I'll shut the hatch again before another big one rolls over us."

"The floor could probably use a wash," Lafayette said. "Although probably not with saltwater. This is going to get sticky. Or gritty. Or something."

"I'm not sure how to go about washing it properly without bringing it back to the dock on the prison island," Tristan said. "It would be really awkward trying to bring buckets of fresh water out to the submarine, even in the cove."

"And even if we had buckets," Lafayette added.

Tristan cut himself off mid-chuckle to duck back down inside the submarine, slamming the hatch shut, presumably just before another wash of water got inside.

"We should be good to get back to the cove now," he decided. "I'm sure Dieter is worrying himself half to death. We should hurry."

"We can take the most direct path, since there's no reason to keep searching now," Lafayette said.

"Isn't there?" Tristan said, even as she settled herself on the lump of a seat and took hold of the controls to get them underway.

"What do you mean? You want to look at more fish?"

She definitely wanted to look at more fish. But

other things had to happen first. The fish would have to wait.

"Well, we know this ship is from an older fleet," Tristan said. "I don't think the ping we saw on the scans from the polar ship was from this one. The other ship, the one from that fleet, still has to be out here somewhere. It's still tied into that systemic field."

"But where else could it be?" Lafayette asked. "This was our most remote search pass, the one all three of us agreed was too far out to be the source of that ping. This was already us just being thorough. What could we have missed?"

Tristan didn't answer. But she knew that wasn't because he didn't agree with her.

It was well past sunset when they finally passed through the phalanx of rock formations and bobbed to the surface of the still waters of the cove. Dieter was waiting for them on the beach, barefoot and fuming. As if they had returned just in time to stop him from swimming out in search of them.

"We found a ship," Lafayette told him at once. "But it's not the right ship."

"Kora thinks it's the original scouting spaceship, the one that found this planet and marked it for the other ships full of settlers to follow,"

Tristan said. "It's definitely a different design. An older one."

"It's also under power, or at least some power," Lafayette said. "The hull had a dim glow to it. Kora thinks it's from the shields still being active."

"We found a few airlocks—" Tristan started to say.

But Dieter was clearly overwhelmed by both of them yammering at him, at high volume and high speed, all but overlapping each other. He held up both hands just to get them to stop. They both fell silent at once.

"One thing at a time," he said. "How deep is it?"

"It took us about ten minutes to reach the surface when we stopped our reconnaissance pass," Tristan said, trading a glance with Lafayette, who added a nod of her own.

"And the submarine will fit inside some part of this spaceship?" Dieter asked. Not quite sarcastically.

"We have the suit," Lafayette said, gesturing in the general vicinity of the submarine in the middle of the cove.

"We need to take some time to think about this," Dieter said. Then he gestured over to their campfire on the beach, the one they had been using all week but banking down during the day.

The flames were low now, but the embers were glowing hotly. "I have some clams baking now. I figured something fresh would be great after nothing but rations for so long."

"I've never had clams before," Lafayette said. But made sure that her tone conveyed her appreciation. Fresh food *did* sound wonderful, even if all their sides would still be freeze-dried bits of whatever they had left in their two stockpiles.

But she was also pretty sure that Dieter had only been barefoot in the water digging up clams because he didn't know what else to do while the wait for their return tormented him. He really had been debating swimming out to find them.

The three of them let the matter of what to do about the spaceship drop long enough to stuff themselves silly with clams and crackers and cheese. Kora fastidiously licked her bowl clean of any trace of her dinner of nutritive paste. Then they all sat back, watching the flames as the first of the moons finally rose into the sky.

"Kora, you were telling me something before about the effects of pressure in deep water," Dieter said at last.

"Oh, yes," Kora said, nudging her bowl aside to turn her attention to Dieter. "In the submarine, we're all fine. And the life support systems on the sunken ship—assuming they're operational, which the light from the active shields tells me they likely are—would also protect us from the effects of pressure."

"And I'm assuming there's no way to get your submarine inside any of those airlocks?" Dieter asked.

"Ah, no," Tristan said with another rub at the back of his neck. "It's too big. And most of the nose of the craft is completely inaccessible to us. That's where the docking bays for shuttles would be, as far from the spinning wheel as possible. It's dark down there and hard to see, but it looks like the nose is jammed into a crevice in the rock. Then the centuries since it came down there have filled the entire area in with silt."

"That's where the shuttle bay would be located," Kora reiterated. "They have to be located well aft of the spinning wheel in the rocket section. Which is just where we can't reach."

"The wheel isn't turning, even though the ship is under power," Lafayette said. "Getting to one of its airlocks shouldn't be a problem. We found several."

"Yeah, but we don't exactly have a way to get out of the submarine and into the ship, do we?" Dieter said.

"But there's the suit," Lafayette said again.

Dieter opened his mouth, but it was Tristan

who got the words in first. "Not that it solves the problem of getting from the submarine to the ship's airlock at all. There's no airlock in the submarine."

"You'd have to get into the suit here, then ride outside of the submarine all the way out to the ship," Dieter said. But musingly, not like he thought it was an insurmountable problem. "You'd have to dive together and stay close to maintain the airflow. Although you'd have to detach the connection to the submarine in order to work the airlock."

"And by 'you', you mean..." Lafayette trailed off.

"Well, *you*. Obviously," he said. "It makes the most sense to stuff you and Kora both inside that suit and send you into that ship. The two of you would fit, whereas with either Tristan or me, we'd have to go solo. Sending a pair is a better idea."

Lafayette nodded and tried to keep her face carefully neutral. But inside, she was already dancing for joy.

"I don't know if the suit was meant for this kind of depth," Tristan said. "My submarine training was barely five minutes of having things pointed out to me. All I got was a point and a quick, 'and that's a diving suit.' Like they assumed I'd never need it."

"They *did* think you were doing this on your own," Lafayette said.

"I need to take a look at it," Dieter said, then got up and dusted the sand off his pants before wading out into the water.

"This maybe isn't worth it," Tristan said to Lafayette in a low voice. "If you're nervous about doing it, I mean. It's a risk we don't have to take."

"But we've pretty much done everything we can to find the other ship, haven't we?" Lafayette said. "If my father got my message at all, I have to know. If he sent a response, I have to get it. I *have* to."

"If the shields are active, communications are likely active too," Kora said. "Although it might need a manual restart of systems, like with the last ship trapped in the ice."

"Once I'm on the ship, I'll be fine," Lafayette said. "Nothing there that I haven't done before."

"We have food for a few days yet," Tristan said. "Especially if Dieter can keep finding us more clams."

"The clams were good," Lafayette agreed.

Then they heard the sound of Dieter splashing his way back to them. "It's definitely showing its age, like the rest of the submarine, but I think this suit is going to work for us."

"I still can't really swim," Lafayette felt compelled to point out. "And that suit looks so bulky."

"You won't need to swim much," Dieter said. "It's more designed for hopping around on the ocean bed, not proper swimming. I have some thoughts on propulsion… but let me noodle on that later. For now, the hoses that connect you to the submarine can be closed off, which was what I really needed to see. That means you can get inside the airlock and close the hoses before disconnecting. That way you don't backwash into the submarine and flood it."

"But then there's no air?" Lafayette said.

"If the airlock works, it will vent the water and bring in ship air almost instantaneously," Kora told her. "You'd only have to hold your breath for a few seconds."

"Not even that," Dieter said. "There'd be enough in the suit with you to sustain you for that length of time. And if the airlock doesn't work, you just hook the hoses back up and restart the connection."

"I'll have to do that anyway, when I come back out," Lafayette said.

"We were just talking and we're assuming that once Lafayette and Kora get inside, they'll stay there until the work is done," Tristan told him. "Hours or days, whatever."

"I don't want to be this far away from her," Dieter said, looking around the island with a frown.

"No, I'm thinking I'll just surface when I need air, but otherwise stay down until she's done. As close as I can keep the submarine," Tristan said. "There is a section of spoke that's almost level. I can drop the anchors on that when I need rest."

"I can keep circling the airship without landing," Dieter said.

"For days?" Lafayette pressed.

"If I have to," he said, raising his chin at her, daring her to argue with him. When she refused to take the bait, he just added, "I'm the king of cat naps. And the weather has never been less than fine since we got here."

"Well, that was kind of true in the north as well," Tristan pointed out. "Right up until that blizzard trapped us there."

"We knew that blizzard was coming days before it hit," Dieter said. "I'm watching the weather patterns just as closely here. We're fine."

"I want to do this," Lafayette said. "I need to know if my father is still up there. If he can hear me. I need to know he knows I'm still coming after him."

"I know," Dieter said. "We'll get you in there. I just hope nothing is so old that not even Kora can read the manuals and figure out the instructions. Because our time really is growing short."

Lafayette knew that was true. She could feel it in her bones. And, not for the first time in the last few days, she found her eyes sweeping the horizon. Always she was watching for any sign of stars blotted out. Of airships quietly closing in on them.

They were safe for now. But now wasn't going to last forever.

CHAPTER 8

Dieter and Tristan stayed up late into the night debating the suit design, but when Lafayette woke in the morning, they had to report they hadn't worked out a good way to get her inside of it out in the middle of the ocean. She had assumed that would be true, but it was still a bit disappointing. It would've been nice, spending a few more hours with Tristan inside the submarine before plunging alone into the unknown.

But it wasn't meant to be. Instead, Lafayette let the other two assist her in climbing inside the bulky, awkward suit. And she needed both of their help to do it. It was heavy, and far too large for her. But she got her feet in the legs, then held

Kora in her arms close to her chest as Dieter and Tristan pulled the body of the suit up to rest on her shoulders.

There was a lot of sag to it. And she didn't bother trying to put her arms into the sleeves at all. She had to hold onto Kora, or the dog's weight would pull the whole thing down again.

"We need to lock the helmet on and secure it," Dieter told her.

"Okay," Lafayette said.

"It'll be hard to communicate once that's on," he said, then turned away as he fussed at something on the helmet exterior.

"Oh," Lafayette said, finally understanding him. Then she looked at Tristan, and tried not to let the anxiety that she didn't know when she'd see him again twist her stomach up too much.

"It's going to be fine," Tristan assured her.

"I don't think, even if I put my arms in the sleeves, that I'd be able to get my hands into those gloves," she said.

Tristan grabbed one as if feeling its weight. "Yeah, it's going to be a challenge."

"We're not going to be close enough to the bottom for me to bounce on my feet, and swimming is out of the question," Lafayette said.

"You only need one hand to hold the propeller," Dieter said, indicating the contraption he had been up early putting together for her. It looked like one of the smaller directional propellers he used to control the airship, but sealed under what appeared to be an enormous quantity of tape.

"You squeeze it to fire it up, then direct it in whatever direction you need to be away from," he said. "You'll get the hang of it, I'm sure."

Lafayette doubted that a lot, but she just shifted Kora to where she could hold her with only her left arm, then thrust her right arm into the sleeve of the suit. Tristan and Dieter both helped her work enough of the bulky fabric back out of her way so she could get her hand into the glove.

Then Dieter lashed the propeller to that glove with a lot more of that tape.

"I don't think this is going to work," Lafayette said.

"It feels awkward now, but it's going to be different when you're in the water," Dieter said, slapping her shoulder with such force that she nearly toppled forward.

"If it's too awkward, we can always abort," Tristan said.

"But I won't be able to talk to you," Lafayette pointed out.

"Follow your hose like a tether back to the submarine," Dieter said, picking up the helmet once more and approaching her with it. "Tristan will know what that means."

"Yeah. It'll be obvious," Tristan said.

"How do I detach the hose when I reach the airlock?" Lafayette asked, looking at the propeller contraption that was already a dragging weight at the end of her arm.

"I wrapped the tape around your wrist, so you can squirm your fingers out from under the trigger to get to the hose," Dieter said. "It attaches to the belly of your suit, in easy reach."

"Press in and twist," Tristan said, demonstrating as he attached it to her front, then detached it before attaching it again.

"Close it off first," Dieter grumbled.

"Right," Tristan said, flushing. "That's this ring here. Make sure it clicks in the locked position before you detach the hoses."

"Or you'll flood the submarine," Dieter said.

"Well, I think I could get to the surface in time to avoid that," Tristan said.

Dieter just raised a single skeptical eyebrow.

"Is this a bad idea?" Lafayette asked in a tiny voice.

"Absolutely not," Dieter said, and put the helmet down over her head. Tristan reached in at the last moment to make sure her hair buns were tucked in, out of the way of the seal.

"Are we really doing this?" Lafayette whispered to herself.

But it was Kora who answered her. "Of course. Going inside ships. It's what we do."

"That's true," Lafayette admitted.

She felt Dieter slap the outside of her helmet and decided that meant he had inspected her seals and deemed her good to go.

She shifted her weight to face the water, but it took Dieter and Tristan both holding on to one of her arms each to get her stumbling towards the submarine. The deeper the water got, the more of a slog this was.

Until they got shoulder-deep, almost at the depth where the submarine waited. Then her air-filled suit finally found a little buoyancy.

Tristan gave her one last thumbs-up before climbing into the submarine and closing the hatch. Dieter remained by Lafayette's side, double-checking the places where the hose attached to the side of the submarine. Then, one hand holding onto the submarine, he used the other to mime taking a deep breath.

Lafayette took three. She could feel a slight breeze over her belly. The connection was good. But the helmet was too heavy for her to give Dieter a nod, and a thumbs-up was entirely out of the question. She had to settle for a heavily enunciated "okay" so he could read her lips.

He nodded, then demonstrated something else he had taped onto her right glove: a metallic hook. He slipped it through a rung next to where her hose attached, then waited for her to attempt to get her own hand free. It was awkward, but she did it. Then he waited as she got it hooked again on her own. Even more awkward. But it would work.

Dieter nodded in satisfaction. Then he slapped the outside of her helmet one last time, slapped the exterior of the submarine, then dove into the water to swim back towards the shore and his waiting airship.

Lafayette realized she was holding her breath and forced herself to breathe normally as Tristan got the submarine underway.

There was a moment of panic when the submarine dragged her head underwater, but it felt far more natural being completely submerged in that suit. And the hook that attached her to its side was holding strong.

So she just hugged Kora tightly and enjoyed the ride.

The helmet was large, even for a full grown man. But while it had been headache-inducingly heavy in the air, underwater it floated around her. And she quickly realized that while the submarine just had the one small window at the front for navigation, this helmet had been designed for exploration. She turned her head to the left and to the right, but there was no direction where she couldn't see out of it. The glass panes ran almost all the way to the back. She had an unimpeded view of everything.

But, alas, no sketchbook. They had moved all of those out of the submarine as well. It felt safer, keeping them in the airship. Not that Lafayette thought she was going to do anything that would flood the submarine. But still.

She would just have to commit everything to memory until she had time with her journals later. Although the rainbow-colored variety of fish that swam all around her was overwhelming her senses. She had only caught glimpses of this from the submarine, and that had been amazing enough. This visual feast? She was never going to remember even half of it.

She would definitely have to come back here someday. When the world was calmer and she had time for proper study.

Surely that day would come.

It took a few hours to get back out to the ship. Lafayette had a pack on her back filled with her share of the remaining supplies, and a few more snacks tucked away in the pockets of her pants as well as a smaller bottle of water. But she wanted to wait as long as possible before touching any of that, as much as her stomach was already growling and her mouth was growing parched.

As awkward as physical needs had been inside the tiny submarine, she didn't have any idea what she could do inside this suit if she had to go. It was roomy, but not that roomy. And she was, as she was all too aware, sharing that suit with Kora.

Tristan kept the submarine just under the surface of the water for most of the trip, which let Lafayette admire the way the sun danced through the water, reflecting off the sides of the fish around her.

But then they reached the underwater canyon, and he started to go deeper. Not steeply, just a gentle angling down towards where he knew the ship would be.

And Lafayette realized there was another way the suit wasn't like the submarine. It had no source of heat. The thickness of the suit fabric was a bit of an insulator, but she could already feel the cold of the deeper water seeping in to where she was hugging Kora.

"It will be warmer on the ship, right?" Lafayette said.

"If the life support systems are running at minimum, it will be chilly but tolerable," Kora told her. "Of course, once we're on board, we can bring the levels back up to a more comfortable zone."

"Yeah, but that takes days," Lafayette said, remembering when they had done the same inside the ship trapped in ice.

"Indeed," Kora said. "We'll find you a sweater."

Lafayette laughed at that.

They continued down into the darkness, and Lafayette realized that ,while she could just see the lights from the submarine doing their best to cut through the murk ahead of them, if her suit had a light of its own, it wasn't currently on. And she didn't know how to reach it if she had one. Her one usable hand was keeping her hooked to the submarine.

But before that could make her too nervous, the wheel of the ship started to emerge from the darkness, and she remembered that the shields had a soft glow. That would be enough to see by. And once she was inside the ship, the emergency lights would be on.

She was going to be okay.

Tristan brought the submarine up close to one of the airlocks, then brought their momentum to a halt. Now they were floating. Floating and drifting ever so slightly towards the north, as the canyon had a gentle current running through it.

"That's it, then," Lafayette said. "It's go time."

"Go time," Kora agreed.

Lafayette floated one huge boot up to the side of the submarine to brace against it. Then she unhooked herself from the side of the vehicle. She did it so smoothly one would think she'd been doing this every day of her life.

She pushed off from the submarine, turned her body around in an eel-like maneuver, then thrust her right hand out behind her before squeezing the trigger of the propeller.

This went a little less like she'd had a lifetime of experience with it. But after a few jerking course corrections, she had it worked out.

And she and Kora were torpedoing through the water to the rectangle of light that framed their destination.

CHAPTER 9

It took ten tries for Lafayette to catch onto the exterior of the airlock door. Ten tries where she knew Tristan was watching her flailing about in the water. It was deeply embarrassing. More than that, she hated the idea that he might be panicking just watching her. She didn't want to cause him any worry on her behalf. And yet, she just couldn't get the clumsy glove fingers to articulate enough to grab on to anything.

Then she remembered the hook Dieter had made for her. Of course he had designed it for this as well as holding on to the submarine.

Grumbling about her own stupidity under her breath, Lafayette used the propeller to turn herself around to start an eleventh approach.

It took two more tries to get it, but finally she was there, hooked onto the exterior of the door. Then she had to move the suit through the water until the controls for the door were in front of her helmet.

"The panel is dead," Lafayette said. She let go of Kora and poked at the panel through the layers of material of the chest of her suit, but nothing responded to her prodding.

"Hmm," Kora said. "We'll need to use the manual entry."

"I can't pry our way inside," Lafayette said, thinking of the last two ships she had been inside. One her father had broken into, using a pry bar. She hadn't seen that happen, but having pushed that door open again to follow him, she knew it hadn't been easy.

She had watched Dieter do the same at the polar ship after they'd finally chipped all the ice away. That definitely hadn't been easy.

She wasn't as strong as Dieter was, not by a long shot. And she was underwater in a bulky suit that made everything twice as difficult as it should be.

And she didn't have a pry bar.

"The emergency systems are still up," Kora told her confidently. "There will be a red lever, oversized to accommodate the gloves of space-walking suits. They're almost as bulky as this one, so I'm sure you'll be fine."

Lafayette double-checked that the hook holding her in place was secure, then gently floated the suit around until she saw the lever Kora was talking about. It was, indeed, oversized.

"I don't want to unhook from the door if I can help it," Lafayette said, imagining another dozen attempts to get back to where she was now if she did. "But I think I can throw that lever with a foot."

Which took a bit of doing. The suit moved better in the water than it had on shore, but bending at the waist with Kora tucked up against her was not really possible. So she had to work by feel, dragging one metal-soled boot against the side of the ship until her toes caught the lever. Then, again by feel, she pushed against the lever, trying to drive it down.

It didn't want to move at first. But then it gave way with an explosive jolt.

"Get inside then detach the hoses," Kora told her.

"Right," Lafayette said. She worked with what she was sure to Tristan's watching eyes must look like exaggerated slowness, getting her legs inside the airlock before detaching the hook, then pushing herself into the metal space. There was a light coming from within, some source she couldn't discern, but it was a soft glow no brighter than the shields outside.

"Close off the air before you detach," Kora reminded her.

"I remember," Lafayette said, but she was far from annoyed that Kora was talking her through the steps. She was so nervous her hands were shaking. But she felt the click just like Dieter had described. Then she pushed in towards her own stomach and twisted. That took a couple of tries, but she got it in the end.

She reached outside of the airlock before gently releasing the hoses. As she hoped, they floated there without moving away from her reach. Depending on how long she ended up being inside, that almost certainly wouldn't be true when she came back. But she still had her propeller, and they couldn't get all that far away with Tristan maintaining his position.

Lafayette looked into the submarine lights, but all she could see was that light. She didn't even get a sense of the window where Tristan must be watching her from. Still, she raised her one workable hand in salute before pulling herself back inside the airlock, mostly out of his sight.

"What now?" she asked.

"Another red lever, but this one between the two doors," Kora told her.

If the dog was frustrated with not being able to see anything but the dank interior of the suit, her voice didn't show it.

Lafayette looked around, found the lever, then found another rung to hook onto so she could repeat her kicking maneuver.

Then everything happened so fast it was a blur. The door she had just opened slammed shut again, and all the water rushed out of the metal box. Her hook lost its hold on the rung, and she was battered around in a whirlpool of evacuating water, but that was all over before she quite understood what was happening.

Then she was on her one hand and both knees, heavy helmet dragging her head down to the floor so that it was nearly impossible for her to sit up. Although that floor was itself at a bit of an angle, maybe as much as thirty degrees from horizontal.

"What now?" Lafayette said, struggling to lift her head. The ill-fitting helmet was rattling around her neck and shoulders too much. The weight of it kept shifting awkwardly.

"Now we take the helmet off and get out of the suit," Kora said. She sounded downright chipper. Well, who could blame her? It had to be worse inside this suit for her than it was for Lafayette.

"Are we sure we can breathe this?" Lafayette asked. They both ignored the fact that Kora, being partly robot, could get by with far less oxygen than Lafayette needed.

"The airlock manual systems functioned as they were meant to," Kora told her. "The water was forced out of here because air was coming in. Everything is working just like it's designed to."

Lafayette supposed that was true. Still, it was the hardest thing she'd ever done, reaching up with her one gloved and taped hand to find the helmet catch and open the seal.

The air that rushed in to wash over her face was cold but fresh and sweet, like glacial water. She drank in a few grateful lungfuls, then got to work getting herself and Kora out of the suit.

There was one more lever to get inside the ship proper, but this time she had two hands to pull it with. She left the suit inside the airlock, hoisted up the straps of the pack she was carrying on her back, and led the way inside the ship.

The air inside the ship was warmer than it had been inside the other ship that had been trapped in polar ice when they found it, but that wasn't saying much.

It also smelled clean. Not just lacking the tell-tale scents of dying things, because even if the crew had died down here, that had been so many centuries ago those smells would have long since gone stale.

No, it was that very staleness that was missing. No musty smell, no mildew smell. It was just… fresh. Not quite scented, but still very, very clean. It didn't have the long-abandoned smell the polar spaceship had had.

"The life support systems are clearly on, if only on minimal settings," Kora told her, clearly watching Lafayette just sniffing the air over and over again. "It's warmer in here than the water temperature outside, and the scrubbers have been keeping the air fresh."

"I still need to find a sweater or something," Lafayette said, but took a moment before she left the vicinity of the airlock to find the control panel. Unlike its exterior counterpart, this panel was fully functional. She carefully read the script for each of the menu options until she found the command to turn the lights around the airlock on or off. She toggled it back and forth a few times, the best she could do to let Tristan know she was safely inside.

"We'll come back to do that again just before sunset," Lafayette said to Kora as they started walking along what was meant to be the wall of the awkwardly sloped hallway. "Just so he doesn't worry too much."

They paused at the first doorway into what was a private cabin with bunks and storage cabinets built into the walls that flanked the long, narrow living space. It was cold, and she really wished she had some kind of sweater. But she could tell at a glance that this room had been stripped of anything useful. The mattresses were bare, and the drawers built into the walls were half open and clearly empty.

"It wasn't a crash, then," Lafayette said to Kora as they walked towards the nearest spoke to the center of the ship. It was close to where they were, so the slope wouldn't change much, and the spokes were designed to be walkable on any surface, whether wall, floor, or ceiling. The body of the ship was nose-down at a forty-five degree angle, but Lafayette had climbed through worse.

"Yes, it does look like they took everything with them when they left," Kora agreed. "Although how they got out of here, I can't imagine."

"They left the systems running," Lafayette said. "Like they thought they'd be coming back."

"And yet they never sent word back to the rest of us in the fleet," Kora said. "I wonder what happened to them?"

"Maybe we can find some books somewhere," Lafayette said, although she wasn't hopeful. When her ancestors stripped a place bare to leave it behind, they really stripped it bare. All of her explorations so far had only yielded a single reader, after all.

They followed the spoke of the wheel in towards the center of the ship. In the other ships Lafayette had been on, the spokes had ended at a level that had been administrative, with classrooms and the brig among other things. But in this ship, the spoke ended directly in the engineering section of the ship. And that section, built around the central drive core, ran for more decks than Lafayette could count in the dim light.

But she could see the soft glow of that core far below her, hibernating in low-energy mode.

"Do we find the bridge?" Lafayette said to Kora. "I mean, everything can be controlled from there, but we could also bring up the heat and everything from here. Although, to be honest, what I absolutely want to do first is see if my father got my message."

"The bridge might be further aft—or, I guess, down now—than we really have to go," Kora said. "There must be a communications station closer. Let's check that sign."

"Sure, do the smart thing," Lafayette said with a fond smile down at her always-thinking dog. Then she picked her way over to the sign that

Kora's sharper senses had seen from across the tilted engineering room.

The letters were strange, the font more elaborate than Lafayette was used to reading, but she could understand it with a little focused attention.

"Correspondence room?" Lafayette said, pointing to one part of the sign with a questioning frown.

"That's it," Kora said. "It's where the crew of the fleet ships go to send messages to friends and family on other fleet ships. Not as elaborate as the communications station on the bridge, but we're not trying to send a signal across interstellar space or anything. Let's see if it's working."

Lafayette double-checked the directions on the sign, then led the way down another corridor.

Climbing around a space that was set at a forty-five degree angle was exhausting, as almost nothing was level at that orientation. It was a lot of bracing herself with one foot on each side of a corner and making her way slowly to avoid twisting an ankle.

Luckily, this part of her day's journey, she had done before.

They reached the correspondence room and found the communication console lit up and functioning. But there was no way to sit in that chair, not when it faced down at a forty-five degree angle. So Lafayette had to find a way to squat over the console itself, but carefully to be sure she wasn't standing on anything important.

She scrolled through the cache of incoming messages, but if she was reading the dates correctly, which she was sure she was, everything was centuries old.

"This might be historically interesting, to have copies of all these messages," Lafayette said with a sigh, even as she kept scrolling, "but there's nothing here from my dad."

"No, that makes sense," Kora said. "This ship wasn't part of that fleet's systemic field. It didn't receive what you sent out to all the other ships in that field, and it didn't receive your father's response."

"But it *could*, right? I mean, we can find a way to get a signal through?" Lafayette said. "We got all the way here. And, miracle of miracles, this thing isn't even broken. There must be something we can do."

"Check the settings," Kora said, gesturing with her nose towards the button that would open that screen.

"And?" Lafayette said, even as she pushed the button. "The default for this station is fleet-wide, but this ship isn't part of the fleet we're trying to reach. I don't think it's part of any fleet at all."

"It was a scout ship, so you're right about that," Kora said, peering down at the settings screen. "See if you can change it to something like 'all ships in the area'."

"All ships in the area?" Lafayette repeated. "Doesn't that include anything that Central Planning controls? Every station with comms, every airship, every… everything they have."

"Yes, that's true," Kora said. "But you won't be transmitting. You'll just be checking for messages. They might not notice."

"Might not," Lafayette repeated. No way was she betting everything on a "might not." She sighed, then settled a little deeper into her squat on her heels. She absolutely was not going to rush this.

"Okay, here's another option," she said after a few quiet moments of clicking through setting screens. "I can ping a specific ship. It says it will bring up a list of all active communication system consoles in range. That range is the entire planet, and surrounding space out past both of the moons. Will Central Planning know if I do that? Just a directed ping?"

"They won't sense this ship searching for other ships," Kora said after a moment's thought. "And provided you ping one specific console and not every console in the area, they shouldn't sense that either. But you have to be sure it's the right one. There will be many."

"Well, I think that part will actually be easy," Lafayette said, pushing the button to scan for active consoles. Kora wasn't wrong, the list was indeed enormous. She watched the address numbers first fill her screen then force the top lines to keep scrolling as new lines were added to the bottom. But she pushed a different button before it had even reached the end. She had what she needed.

The button she had pushed changed the screen view. Now those same console addresses were no longer long chains of numbers; they were pinpoints on a map. Some were worryingly close to their position, although all those dots as she watched them just seemed to be meandering around in a loose circular pattern centered around what she was sure was the prison island. Flying patrols or something similar.

Then she zoomed out the map and pointed to the screen to show Kora what she meant. "There's only one console currently in motion higher than airships can fly. That's my father's ship, up in orbit. It *has* to be, right?"

"Right," Kora agreed with a nod. "Ping it, and it will ping back. That will sync this console's recent message cache with the one on that ship.

Your message should still be in its cache, since it was in the same systemic field where you sent it from."

Lafayette sent the ping, then waited.

She didn't have to wait long. A single message came back to her.

It wasn't her own message. It was something newer. She checked the timestamp and saw it had been sent just hours after the time she knew she had sent her own message, so many days before.

It was from her father. It had to be.

CHAPTER 10

Lafayette stared at the incoming message on the console screen, unable to bring herself to touch it.

She had learned to read the information that messages were labeled with by the communication system during the days they had spent on the bridge of the ship trapped under the ice. She knew the location was correct for her father's ship. It was the same data she had used when she had sent her message to him.

And she knew she wasn't reading the timestamp wrong either. He must've gotten her message some time after she sent it, or took some time to compose his response before sending it. Either way, a few hours' delay wasn't strange. For all she knew, he was still trapped in his cell in the brig on the spaceship. The teaching construct she had left running—the one of Frank Paine who had taught the higher-level classes when the ship had been full of people—would have had to bring the message to him then convey his response if he were indeed still trapped.

She would know just what had happened to him since she saw him last. All she had to do was press the playback button.

"Lafayette?" Kora said, looking up at her with those wise human eyes in her kind doggy face.

"I'm ready," Lafayette said, and jabbed the button with her fingertip.

The speakers in the console blared to life in a cacophony of chaotic sound, but it was a crescendo that was over and done with before Lafayette could even react, let alone find the button to shut it down.

"What was that?" Lafayette asked. It had been so loud that her ears were still ringing.

"There is a tiny possibility it was a corrupted file," Kora said. "The systems on the fleet ships are quite old. And this one is older still."

"But you don't think so," Lafayette said. Her hands were already reaching for the straps of her pack, hiking it a little higher on her shoulders. She felt like sprinting was about to be called for. She was already shaking from the first hits of adrenaline.

"No, I think that was a trap," Kora said. "They knew you'd try to retrieve messages from that ship. I don't know how they did it, but they left this program disguised as a message. Oh, Lafayette. I'm quite sure that means they know we're here."

"Yeah," Lafayette said, punching her way back to the screen where she had searched for all neighboring consoles.

The meandering dots, one by one, changed their headings. They were closing in on her. And the ship.

And Dieter and Tristan. Only they didn't even know that danger was coming.

"I'm going to warn them," Lafayette said, switching from the part of the console for sending and receiving recorded messages to the part that sent out live transmissions.

"Even if you encrypt it, they'll know it's from you, here and now," Kora said.

"I'm not going to bother trying to encrypt anything," Lafayette said. "They already know both those things, so no point in hiding now. No, we have to run. All of us."

She keyed on the microphone and said, as calmly as she could despite the adrenaline making her voice want to go all jittery, "Dieter. Tristan. Company coming. Run. Hide."

Then, without waiting for a response, she hopped down from the console and raced back through engineering to the spoke that would take her back to the airlock and her waiting suit.

She had no idea how many of the dots of active consoles she had seen on the screen had been from communications systems on airships, how many on conventional ships, or how many had been on that new fleet of submarines. But she would guess there was a mix of all three of those things closing in on them now.

If there was a single cloud in the sky, Dieter would find a way to hide in it. He was very good at that.

But Lafayette wasn't sure what Tristan's options would be. She hoped he didn't try sinking down to the bottom of the canyon. That might remove him from the sight of Central Planning, but she really didn't like the idea of him trying that maneuver in that old submarine with all of its ominous creaks and pops.

No, it would be better for him to snuggle in as close as he could where one of the ship's spoke met the wheel. Just where he said he was going to anchor down at night, in fact. The soft light from the active shields might be enough to hide him.

But he couldn't stay down there forever. And when he surfaced for air, he was going to be findable by any of Central Planning's ships.

Lafayette had to force her worrying mind to stop focusing on Tristan now. She had warned him, and he was clever. He would figure something out, likely something she wasn't even thinking of.

But in the meantime, she had herself and Kora to get to safety. And that was going to be a lot trickier.

The running warmed her up enough so that by the time the two of them reached the airlock, she was no longer feeling the cold. But her hands were shaking, anyway. Even after the running, she had too much adrenaline still coursing through her. Her fingers fumbled at the bulky suit, and she had to force herself to spend a couple of precious minutes just breathing and slowing her racing heart.

"Use your hover disks for a minute, will you? I need both my hands," she said to Kora, who readily obliged. Lafayette caught the floating dog and tucked her inside her own shirt to keep her close to her chest. Then she started wiggling her way back inside the heavy suit.

It felt like it took forever, getting back inside that suit. But she kept her breathing slow and steady, focusing on one task at a time and not any of the thousands that were piling up after it. She kept her anxiety carefully in check. And when she finally reached the task that was putting her helmet on and sealing it up, her hands were steady enough that even through the bulky glove she only needed three tries to get it done.

"This was a shorter trip than we thought, right?" she said to Kora.

"Perhaps we can come back later," Kora said brightly.

Lafayette doubted that very much. She had hoped the same about the last spaceship she had been forced to leave behind. And Central Planning had sunk that to the bottom of the polar sea. Once they followed her signal to this ship's location, its days were sadly numbered.

And they wouldn't even bother trying to study any of its secrets first. Destroying any sign of their ancestors seemed to be all Central Planning was ever interested in.

Destroying the past so they could keep rewriting the present to suit them.

Lafayette, the daughter of a historian and archaeologist, hated them for that. And she *would* find a way to stop them.

But first, she had to get herself safely out of their reach.

She kicked the lever to reverse the airlock procedure from before. Now the room filled with water, a little slower than it had evacuated it before. Or maybe it was just the adrenaline messing with her sense of the flow of time.

Then the door slid open, and she was looking out into the impenetrable murk of the deep ocean. There was nothing before her eyes. The glow from the ship's shields vaguely illuminated her peripheral vision, but nothing was in front of her.

There was no sign of Tristan and the submarine. So he had gotten her message and fled as she had told him to.

But there was also no sign of her air hose. And that she hadn't counted on. At all. And she really should have.

"What now?" she said, clicking her tongue against her teeth as she pondered her options.

"Up," Kora said. "Use the propeller Dieter gave you and get us up. It's either that or go back inside the ship."

Lafayette traded clicking her tongue for biting down on her lip. Because retreat was starting to sound like the safer option.

But it was the same as with the polar ice ship. She could stay safe inside it, basically for*ever*. But she would be safely trapped inside. She wouldn't be able to get to her father from there.

And she wouldn't be able to help her friends.

"Right," she said at last, wrapping an arm around Kora inside the suit, then jumping out of the airlock and thrusting her right hand with the propeller lashed to it behind her.

She squeezed its trigger with all her might and tried to streamline the rest of her body as much as she could.

Kora said nothing, and Lafayette slowly realized that the dog was holding her breath. She was leaving all the air for Lafayette. The instant she recognized this, Lafayette focused on her own breathing. She couldn't hold it for anywhere near as long as Kora could. But she could keep her breathing controlled. She calmed her mind, slowed her breathing and her heartbeat, and kept her head tipped back so she could see out the forehead section of the oversized helmet.

Nothing but darkness above. She had left the glow of the ship behind, but now she was lost in a world of inky blackness. She knew she was moving, but she couldn't see it. She couldn't even feel it.

But she had to believe it. The propeller in her hand was doing something.

Her brain was getting muddy, confused, so at first she wasn't sure exactly what she was seeing. There was light directly in front of her, she was sure of it. But if it was the surface of the water she was approaching, shouldn't it be light everywhere? And yet it looked like such a pinpoint.

A pinpoint surrounded by blossoming pools of blackness. Oh. That was her vision tunneling. She was going to pass out. She didn't have enough air left inside the suit to sustain her.

But she was so close.

She closed her eyes, hugged Kora close, and put all of her will into keeping her hand with the propeller steady. The light would be there. She just had to stay alive long enough to reach it.

Her head got suddenly heavier, and there was a moment's panic about what this new symptom could possibly mean. But that panic had her eyes flying open, and she saw the sun in a cloud-free blue sky all above her. Waves were slapping against the glass sides of her helmet, knocking it about. It was heavier because it was half out of the water.

Her instincts wanted to suck in a deep breath now that she was out of the water, only there still wasn't any air for her to suck in. She was still trapped inside that helmet.

She fumbled at the seal, breaking it open on the first try. But the helmet immediately started to fill with water.

And then, so did the suit.

Lafayette barely caught a breath before her head was under the waves again. Under the waves, and going down, all the way back down to the deep.

She felt Kora float up past her, heading for the surface under her own steam. Lafayette felt a spasm in her chest at the abandonment of her companion, but she quickly realized this was actually a good thing.

Without Kora in the suit with her, she could more easily slip out of it herself. Then she slipped the straps off her shoulders and let her backpack sink down after it. There was nothing in it but food and water, anyway. Without air, neither of those things mattered.

Free of encumbrances, Lafayette could finally move both her arms as well as her legs. She focused on every brief swimming lesson that Tristan and Dieter had given her in their long nights in the cove and focused on stroking her way up through the water that pressed painfully against her eardrums.

She swam as best she could. She swam for all she was worth.

This time, when her head broke through the waves, she could finally suck in all the air she liked. The waves still pummeled her mercilessly, and she sputtered and spat out saltwater between breaths, but it was still so delicious just to pull oxygen out of the air.

Kora floated up to her, wedging her body under Lafayette's arms. Her robot body was heavy, Lafayette knew that from personal experience. Her hover disks must be firing at full power to keep her on the surface. And now she was using some of that precious power to keep Lafayette afloat as well.

"There's Dieter," Kora said, and Lafayette finally shifted her attention away from the joys of breathing to look back up into the blue sky again. It took her a moment to find the glint of light in the sky that gave away Dieter's position. He wasn't directly overhead, and Lafayette rather doubted he was close enough to see her and Kora down amongst the waves.

Then she realized that he almost definitely didn't see her, maneuvering as he was to avoid a trio of airships. That would take all his attention.

The airship they had stolen from Stewart after he had taken it from Margo was the best airship in the Central Planning fleet. If he had still been in his family's older model airship, he never would've even been able to attempt the kind of flying he was doing now.

But Lafayette knew from what she'd seen on the console screen that more airships were coming. Not even he would be able to keep avoiding capture when those ships arrived.

He needed to fly away from here. He needed to leave her behind. But he wasn't doing it. He was staying close.

And even if she found a way to flail her arms at him and he actually saw her, she doubted he would leave just at her say-so.

"Lafayette!" Kora cried, and Lafayette changed the direction of her beating feet to pivot her body around.

There was a ship pulling up to them. Or maybe the proper word was more like boat: it was scarcely larger than Tristan's submarine, if only designed to float on the surface of the water.

Lafayette made a half-hearted attempt to swim back, away from the outstretched arms of the people on the boat. But there was no way. She could see now other boats approaching, and if her only option was to dive back down, she really had no options at all.

She and Kora were hauled out of the water and tossed onto the sun-warmed boards of the deck. Lafayette scrambled to throw her arms around Kora, then folded her up inside her legs as well. No one was taking her dog from her without a fight.

Then a middle-aged woman in a black Central

Planning uniform was kneeling in front of her, shining a light directly in her eyes.

"Headache?" she barked at Lafayette.

At first Lafayette thought this officer was accusing *her* of being a headache. But then she saw the patch over the name tag on her uniform, a simple equal-armed cross. This officer was a medic.

"Yeah," Lafayette said. The sunlight reflecting off the water and everything else all around her was stabbingly bright, and the backs of her eyeballs were throbbing with each stab.

"We need to get her back to base at once," the officer snapped at one of the other men standing on the boat.

"But we still haven't—" he started to object, but the woman cut him off with the sharp motion of one hand.

"Central Command says we can put her in the medical stabilizing pod," someone else said. Lafayette's head was getting swimmy again, and her neck hurt too much to keep swiveling her head around to track all the voices.

But she was pretty sure she could guess the end of the one guy's sentence. She thought she knew what they still hadn't done. Or, at least, she hoped she did.

Because it meant they still hadn't found Tristan and his submarine.

Hands grasped her shoulders, and she wriggled away from them, holding Kora even tighter.

"Settle down, kid," the medic said, using a disconcertingly soft voice after all the shouted commands she had been giving. "We're going to put your dog in there with you. I don't know *what* she is, but she's got at least some living tissue left to her. I don't know what the bends might do to her, but she's going in there with you."

Lafayette had about a hundred new questions raised by those few statements, but she had no energy left to ask them. Her whole body was hurting.

"Get inside," the medic said. "I'll help you. You'll feel better once you're in there."

Lafayette forced her eyes to open so she could take one last look around. Dieter was still nearby, outflying five ships now. But there was still no sign of Tristan.

"Lafayette, we need to get inside that pod," Kora said to her. Softly, and not at all muffled by the arms and legs Lafayette had wrapped around her. As much as her snout was buried in Lafayette's armpit, her vocal speaker was not covered.

Lafayette heard the others on the boat gasping

softly at the sound of Kora's voice. Prosthetic limbs, even on dogs, weren't unheard of, especially in the capital.

But computer constructs that talked like people? Those definitely were something none of these people had ever even imagined, let alone known existed. They'd certainly never seen a talking dog.

Lafayette wanted to run away. But, shaky as she was, there was no way she was swimming to safety.

There was definitely something wrong with her, although she didn't understand just what it was. But this woman, this medic, seemed to have some idea.

Kora nudged Lafayette under her chin, and Lafayette gave her one last tight squeeze. Then she climbed across the deck to where the woman and another officer were squatting, holding open what looked like the flaps of a tent.

A very low, very narrow tent with puffy sides.

Like an inflatable coffin.

But Lafayette was too worn out to let even that ghoulish image repel her. She slipped inside as easily as she did into her bedroll at night, and pulled Kora close beside her.

She vaguely heard the sounds of the flaps being closed behind her. She was sealed inside.

Then a puff of air bathed over her face. It smelled like something that reminded her of her mother. A plant she had grown outside their cottage door...

Lavender. It was lavender. And it brought with it so many other impressions. Warm sunlight on the baked earth of her front step. Her mother's voice as she spoke with someone who was consulting her for advice on medicines.

The feeling of being home, and warm and dry, and absolutely safe.

Lafayette closed her eyes, drank in that feeling, and let herself drift off to tired sleep.

CHAPTER 11

Lafayette heard birds calling, the crash of surf in the distance, and even a strange barking sound that seemed familiar, although she couldn't quite place it.

She could smell saltwater, and the sharper aroma of seaweed drying out on sun-warmed sand. But there was also a damper smell, sort of mildewy or mossy, that didn't fit with the other two.

Her whole body ached, but not like it had before. This was more like the first good day after a long illness, when it took a bit of work to get your atrophied limbs moving again. The headache was gone. But the partly furry, partly metallic warmth of Kora's body was still pressed close to her side. So, no reason to panic.

Slowly she opened her eyes to find herself lying on a cot under a very thin blanket. The cot was in a tiny room surrounded on three sides by stone walls. The fourth wall was metal bars from stone floor to stone ceiling, and the outline of a door cut into those metal bars was almost surely locked.

Prison. She was in a prison cell. That explained the familiarity of the sounds. She had heard the same things when hiding in her crate back on the airship.

The airship. The submarine!

Lafayette pushed herself up on her elbows and momentarily regretted it as the world started to wash away from her. But she fought back the urge to faint, and once her vision stopped trying to black out on her, she finished sitting up. But more slowly this time.

"Lafayette!" Kora said, bolting up at the first hint of motion and pressing her nose into Lafayette's face. Her tail was beating loudly against the thin mattress as she licked Lafayette's cheeks.

"I'm okay," Lafayette said, but the words were hard to get out because her mouth was so very sticky.

"They left you food and water on the tray

against the wall there," Kora told her, and Lafayette turned her head to see a plate covered with an opaque plastic dome, and beside it a tall bottle filled with water. It was only two steps from bed to tray, but she only made one of those steps completely upright before going down on her knees to cross the rest of the way.

She felt weak and trembly all over.

"How long was I out?" she croaked at Kora as she unscrewed the cap from the bottle.

"Four days," Kora said. "Be careful with the water. Take it slow."

Lafayette just nodded, then took a careful sip of the water. She let it sit in her mouth for a bit, unsticking the sticky. Then she swallowed it down before taking a second, larger sip.

"They said you were all right, and you were only sleeping because they were sedating you, but I didn't know for sure," Kora said. "Lorna said she had no reason to harm you, and I guess I believed her, but I don't know."

"Lorna is the medic?" Lafayette guessed as she took a third sip of water before turning her attention to the plate of food.

"That's right," Kora said. "She has been… well, I can't say kind exactly. More like… civil."

"I'll take civil," Lafayette said. She lifted the lid and found a strange assortment of fresh food. It was a welcome sight after all the prepackaged food she'd been eating lately. But she wasn't sure what meal this arrangement was meant to be. Lunch, maybe? The apple, cored and sliced, as well as the three peeled but still whole hard-boiled eggs she at least recognized. But the center of the plate featured a large handful of some kind of whitish nut she had never seen before in her life.

She decided one of the apple slices would be the best place to start, mostly because just the sight of the food had started her stomach growling so loudly she was sure that Kora could hear it.

But there didn't seem to be anyone else in earshot.

"Guards?" Lafayette whispered to Kora between munches of apple.

"A few," Kora said, equally low. "I believe they also have cameras to watch us. They know when I move around, at least."

Lafayette made a hum of acknowledgement, then decided her stomach wasn't objecting too badly to her first bites and food, and she could risk trying an egg.

"Dieter and Tristan?" she finally asked. Then braced herself for bad news.

But Kora said, "Oh, they're both here. You slept

inside the pod while they brought us ashore, but I was awake. After they took us out of the water, Dieter followed our boat the rest of the way to the island. Then he landed and just came out and turned himself over to the prison guards."

"He could've run for it," Lafayette said. "His family is out there somewhere, looking for us. He could've gone back to them."

"Maybe," Kora said. Then she pitched her voice lower still, so that Lafayette had to strain to catch the words. "Dieter didn't get captured. He surrendered. He has a plan. He must."

Lafayette was struck again by the unfaltering faith her dog had in Dieter. But she couldn't exactly say it was unfounded.

"And Tristan?" she asked instead.

"He came in later," Kora said. "We were out of the medical pod, then. In some sort of pressure chamber deeper in this building. It was like a medical bay, with dozens of beds and all sorts of equipment for diagnosing and treating injuries. I was in the chamber with you, so I couldn't hear anything, but I could see Tristan through the glass door. And he could see me."

"And he was all right?" Lafayette asked.

"Lorna the medic checked him over for injuries while two guards stood by, and once she was done, they took him away," Kora said. "But he was all right. I suppose he and Dieter both are around here somewhere."

"So we're inside the prison on the island, where we were heading in the first place," Lafayette said.

"Yes. And Margo Weiss is on her way here now," Kora said. "No one is to do anything with her prisoners until she's here to deal with us personally."

Lafayette nodded, but they both knew what Kora really meant. Once Margo was there, her first order would be to take Kora away from Lafayette. For dismantling and study. Which would kill her.

"We have to get out of here before she gets here," Lafayette said. "How much of this place have you seen?"

"Very little," Kora admitted.

"It looks pretty primitive," Lafayette said, running a hand over the stone wall behind her. It was ever so slightly damp but also gritty, like ocean spray was somehow making its way all the way inside to coat and then evaporate away from the walls.

"The medical bay is quite different," Kora said. "In fact, I recognized everything inside of it. It's all exactly what we would have found if we had visited the medical bays on either of the other two ships from the fleet."

"Exactly?" Lafayette stressed.

"Yes, exactly," Kora said. "The third ship that came down here? They must've taken all of that equipment out of it and set it up inside this stone building. But deeper, in the sublevels of the basement. There were many security check points between there and here."

"Maybe they took the communications console and moved it intact as well," Lafayette said. "That would explain why we couldn't find the ship. Because it's not on the ship anymore."

"Perhaps," Kora said.

Lafayette looked at the strange nuts that were all that was left on her plate. Then she looked around for any other bowl or plate inside their cell.

"Your paste," Lafayette said.

"It's still on the airship, I assume," Kora said. "Except for the tube you had on you when we were inside the diving suit. But that was in your pack. Which is now at the bottom of the ocean."

"But they have the airship. They should be able to give you some of your paste," Lafayette said.

"I did explain," Kora said.

"How long has it been? Four days, you said?"

"Since I last ate? Yes, that's correct," Kora said.

"I've been conserving my energy. I can go a few more. If just a few."

Lafayette didn't want to imagine what would happen then, if Kora still didn't get the paste she needed. Would her living dog parts start to die, while her robot parts carried on? It didn't bear thinking about.

"Eat," Kora commanded, nudging Lafayette's hand back towards the nuts. "You need the fats as well as the protein to get your strength back."

"I'm sure they have my meal plan set to stunt that process. It's not like they want me at full strength here," Lafayette said. But she put one of the nuts in her mouth. It had been roasted and salted, and anything was tolerable if it had been roasted and salted. But the actual nut flesh was bitter and astringent. Lafayette took another drink from the water bottle, then put more nuts in her mouth.

"Did you see any of the other prisoners here? The ones who were here before us?" Lafayette asked.

"You mean Uche," Kora said. "No, I haven't seen him. I asked Lorna the medic, but she's not part of the prison guard system, she said. She's support crew for the submarine fleet they're building here. She says she doesn't mix with the prisoners or even the guards. I don't know if I believe her. I've seen her chatting with some of the guards anyway. But she's probably not lying that she doesn't know anything about any of the prisoners."

"It sounds like they really are replacing the prison here with an outpost," Lafayette said. "But why? What's out here that's something Central Planning needs submarines to protect?"

"It's all very mysterious," Kora agreed.

Lafayette finished the last of the nuts. She tried to save some of the water for later, but the astringency of the nuts was too intense. Even after she had drained the last drops from the bottle, there was still a bitter dryness to her tongue.

But once the food was gone, her weariness came back.

"Lean on me," Kora said, nudging herself under Lafayette's elbow. Lafayette steadied herself against the dog's side, then managed to crawl the few steps back to the cot. It was a very low cot, only halfway to knee-height if she had been standing up. Rolling over onto it was the easiest thing in the world.

"Are they still drugging me?" Lafayette mumbled into the pillow. She felt Kora pulling the blanket out from under her, then arranging it over her with little tugs of her mouth.

"No, you're just recovering," Kora told her

softly. Then she turned around once before flopping against Lafayette's stomach. Lafayette put an arm around her and snuggled her close.

"I'll be better after a nap," she said.

She had a moment then to wonder, what was that strange barking sound she kept hearing in the distance? Were there more dogs here? Could she go find them if she got out of this room?

But the monotonous roar of the surf racing up some sandy beach drowned out the barking, or at least her brain just focused on that roar. She could just picture that beach, even though she'd never seen it. She could picture the water rushing up then falling back, over and over again.

Until, finally, it succeeded in lulling her back to sleep.

CHAPTER 12

Lafayette woke some time later to the cold press of Kora's nose against her cheek.

"Quiet," Kora purred to her. "Wake up, but stay quiet."

Lafayette nodded. It was nighttime, but her prison cell was far from totally dark. The row of lights that ran up and down the corridor outside the open bars of her cell was set up high enough into that vaulted ceiling that they didn't shine directly on her cot, but they were always burning. Lafayette had no problem making out the shape of Kora sitting beside her on the cot. And when she sat up she saw the tray of food had been replaced while she had been sleeping.

Lafayette took stock of her readiness to flee.

She was still wearing her own clothes, but they had been laundered at some point before being put back on her. Otherwise they'd be stiff with dried saltwater by now, and she would be unbearably itchy sleeping in such things.

Her pockets were empty, which was probably to be expected. She had her socks on, but not her shoes. She looked around the floor of her cell for her shoes, but they were nowhere in sight.

She was still looking at the floor when a sudden shadow blotted out the light. But she could feel Kora beside her vibrating with happy excitement, and she knew that could only mean one thing.

Dieter. Dieter had come to break her out.

She threw back the blanket to head for the door that she could sense him tinkering with somehow, although with the lights behind him she couldn't see what he was doing. But she made a brief detour to snatch the water bottle up from her tray before following Kora to the door.

Dieter opened the lock with a soft click, then swung the door open with almost exaggerated slowness. It creaked, but just barely. At his raised hand, she and Kora both froze in place, and Lafayette even held her breath.

She saw Dieter's head turn as he looked off to

his right. He gazed that way for what felt like forever.

And then his hand was gesturing again, but this time for her to follow him.

He didn't bother to tell her to be quiet. That was understood.

Her socked feet were soundless on the stone floor, and Kora hovered beside her with her paws not quite touching the ground.

Dieter led them past empty cell after empty cell. Then they turned a corner and went down an even longer brightly lit corridor between empty prison cells. She looked up and could see four more levels of cells above them. But there was no sign of life anywhere.

The corridor ended with a single steel door, which was held ajar by a piece of volcanic rock about the size of a fist. Dieter held the door open for the other two to slip inside, then gently moved the rock out of the way. He guided the door shut so slowly that the click when it was finally in place was all but inaudible.

Lafayette raised her eyebrows at him, silently asking if it was okay to talk in this new space. But he shook his head at her, then waved for her to follow him down a flight of stairs.

The stairs were metallic but not solid. They were like an open grate, and she could see through them to staircase after staircase of the same expanded metal.

They definitely weren't meant for people not wearing shoes, and Lafayette flinched more than once as the exposed edges of the expanded metal dug into the tenderest parts of her feet.

She quickly lost track of how many levels down they went, but it wasn't anything like all the way down. She could still see what appeared to be an infinite number of staircases continuing on below them when Dieter caught her elbow and nudged her towards another open steel door.

The corridor beyond was barely lit by an irregular row of red lights. The floor here was entirely metal, but almost painfully cold through Lafayette's socks. She couldn't make out the ceiling above those dim red lights, but she didn't think it was stone anymore, although the walls in the stairwell had been.

This was something else. If she didn't know better, she would almost think they were inside a spaceship. But it wasn't quite that either. Although when she tried to put her finger on how she knew it wasn't quite that, she couldn't summon up a specific impression as to why. Something just felt… off.

No gentle exchange of air through a life support system, maybe? Or no sense of immense space all around her? It did feel a little claustrophobic, although that might just be because of the darkness too close in all around her.

Dieter caught her elbow again, this time to keep her from continuing down the red-lit hallway past the door he was holding open for her. She backed up the couple of steps she had overshot it, then stepped into a space that she knew at once was small. Like closet-sized small.

Kora hovered in beside her, pressed up close against her. Then Dieter was inside too, jostling them both as he slowly closed the door behind them.

She heard him release a long-held breath, and then a click as he hit a light switch. She had to hold a hand between her eyes and that light for a moment to give her pupils a chance to adjust. But before they'd managed to do that, she felt arms closing in around her.

"I thought I'd lost you," Tristan said, his voice muffled against her hair. "I didn't see you come back out. I thought I'd left you behind."

"No, we made it," Lafayette said. Then she was hugging him back, so tightly she heard him squeak in surprise. But she didn't loosen her embrace even then.

"Kora, good to see you," Dieter said, as dry as ever. Clearly, the two of them embracing were making him uncomfortable. To be fair, it was a very small closet.

Lafayette finally let Tristan go and stepped back. Then she gave Dieter a briefer hug, but still one he hadn't expected from the way he flinched when she touched him.

"Thank you, Dieter," she said. "You could've made it to safety in that airship. I saw you up there and I know you had the upper hand."

"Momentarily," was all he would concede. He patted her shoulder awkwardly, and she let him go. But as they all settled down on the floor, she found her hands tangled up with Tristan's in the small space between them.

She didn't pull hers away.

"Now what?" Tristan said.

"It's been four… no, five days now," Dieter said. "And Margo Weiss is on her way. Which gives us maybe another day before she's here. I heard one of the guards say that Lafayette was finally awake again, so I had to come get you both."

"You say that like you were waiting," Lafayette said.

"I was," Dieter said. "I broke out of my own cell on my first night here. And I've been breaking out again every night since then. I've gotten the lay of the land, so to speak. Everything here at the moment is organizational chaos. This place is technically under the control of Central Planning's naval reconnaissance division. And yet the planned closure of the prison and removal of the last of the prisoners hasn't happened yet."

"There are a lot of empty cells here," Tristan pointed out.

"There used to be a lot more prisoners here," Dieter said. "I've been avoiding the prison part of things, just because the guards over there are ever so slightly more alert than the navy guards on this end."

"Have you seen Uche?" Lafayette asked.

"No, but, like I said, I've been avoiding that area. I wanted to get you both out before we started that kind of search," he said. "We need to have a plan—a good, solid plan—in place before we start messing with breaking out a prisoner."

"The airship is still here?" Tristan asked.

"They haven't even taken anything off it," Dieter said. "I do believe it's considered part of Margo Weiss's responsibility, and no one else wants to touch it."

"Kora's nutritive paste is still there," Lafayette said.

And, she hoped, all of their journals. She really didn't want to start that whole project from scratch again if she didn't have to.

"This good, solid plan you spoke of," Tristan said, "I think a key element to that has to be getting out of here *before* Margo shows up."

"Agreed," Dieter said. "And I would be all for sneaking into the wing with the remaining prisoners and finding Uche Okafo right now."

"Except?" Lafayette said.

"Except I think this place here is what we were looking for," he said, gesturing at the ground beneath their feet. "Not this closet, obviously—"

"The medical bay," Lafayette interrupted him to say. "Kora says the equipment there came from a fleet ship. I'm guessing all of this came from a fleet ship."

"Yes," Dieter said. "I've been up and down all these corridors. The structure is all wrong for a buried ship. It's more like a buried building, with a squared-off shape and level after level all lined up with gravity. But it's not just the central shaft with engineering and the bridge and everything. Most of the top levels here are living quarters. Like from the wheel. But not a wheel frozen in place like we found in the ice in the north. There's no slope here."

"They dismantled the fleet ship *entirely*?" Tristan said.

"Then rebuilt it in this series of subbasements

under the prison," Dieter said. "That's what it looks like to me."

"Where are the remains of the ship?" Lafayette asked.

"Nowhere," Dieter said. "They used every bit here somewhere. They just reshaped what was curved into long horizontal levels. Which couldn't have been that hard to do. Even in the wheel section of the other ship, the ground when you were standing on it felt perfectly flat. You had to walk quite a way to get a sense of a curve to it."

"Or look down the corridor," Tristan mused. "But I could see how breaking it into sections to flatten it out would mask its original shape pretty effectively."

"But why?" Lafayette asked.

"The usual Central Planning reason, I'm sure," Dieter said. "To hide it from the rest of us."

"But it's still operational," Lafayette said. "I mean, obviously it can't *fly*. But the systems are still working."

"The life support has been modified, but it *is* being used to get air from the surface down to here and back again," Dieter said.

"How do you know that?" Tristan asked.

Dieter grinned at them both. "Because I've found the bridge. And all the systems can be controlled or monitored from that bridge. It's all active and running."

"Like the communications console?" Lafayette said.

"And the systemic field controls and navigation systems," Dieter said. "We can't fly, like you said. But we can see so much from here."

"And no one is working down there?" Tristan asked.

"Well, that is the wrinkle in the plan. The new naval people are moving into that space," Dieter said.

"But?" Lafayette said, sensing there was one of those coming.

Dieter turned his grin up a notch as he directed it her way. "So far, they don't have a night shift. We have another six hours from now before anyone at all goes down there."

"Then what are we doing in this closet?" Tristan asked with a laugh.

"Well, there is one little wrinkle," Dieter said. "Not a problem, just a sort of obstacle."

"And that is?" Tristan asked.

"It's forty more levels down," he said. "And there are no lifts. It's staircase after staircase. And all of us, save Kora, are in socks."

"I can take it if you can," Tristan said, lifting his chin at the unspoken challenge. "And apparently you can, because you've been doing this for four nights."

"Hey, the bridge I only found last night," Dieter said. "But point taken. I did have to work my way down there night after night. I think the bottoms of my feet are getting quite tough, actually."

"Did you try looking for shoes?" Lafayette asked, but then waved off the indignant look on his face. "Never mind. I know you did. You're very thorough. Now, shall we start making our way down?"

Because of course she was in a hurry. Somewhere down there was a chance of talking with her father. And she wasn't going to risk another one of those slipping through her fingers.

CHAPTER 13

None of them complained, but Lafayette knew from the sullen quality of the silence between them that they were all nursing wounded feet when they finally reached the bottom of the endless stairwell.

Dieter gestured towards the door without a word, then let Tristan go through first. Lafayette saw Dieter sneaking peaks at the bottoms of his own feet, so she knew not even he was immune to the pain.

The door opened up into a corridor much like the one above, dimly lit only by red lights spaced at the junctions where wall met ceiling. They followed the lights past pair after pair of closed doors.

Then they emerged onto a space they recognized at once as a bridge. The effort to flatten out surfaces in the levels above wasn't followed here. The three levels of the bridge workstations had been moved intact. With the enormous screen dominating the wall which everything was arranged to be facing, it was almost possible to imagine they were on an intact ship.

Dieter settled into the captain's chair, tapping at the controls built into the arms. The screen in front of them all came to life, filled with various bits of information.

"I've been messing with the settings," he admitted with a flush. "That map there shows where the navy guys are right now. It reads their badges, I guess. You can see they're all clustered on the top levels, so we're safe for now."

"And the prison guards?" Lafayette asked.

"They don't have badges, so they're invisible from here," Dieter admitted. "But they're also not allowed on any naval subbasement, not even the med bay. We're fine."

"Communications?" Tristan said, pointing to the console they all knew was the correct one.

"Right," Lafayette said, sliding into the seat in front of it. Nice not to have to squat the entire time, but she wasn't going to let it lure her into relaxing. She needed to stay tense.

"We have five hours before the morning shift comes down here," Dieter said pointedly.

"Yeah," Lafayette said, looking at all the screens without touching anything yet.

"What happened on the ship under the water?" Tristan asked. "Did you get to do anything at all before they grabbed us?"

"Well," Lafayette said, and she could feel the heat as her cheeks flared up to their brightest shade of red. "Okay, they found us then because the message I touched wasn't from my father. It was something that had been programmed to give away my position wherever I opened it. And before I touched it, I could see all the airships and submarines and boats on patrol. It looked like I would assume a patrol should look like. But the minute I opened the message and gave away my location, they all closed in on us at once."

"They didn't seem to show up out of nowhere in a big hurry," Dieter said. "I'm starting to think we never tricked them at all when we first arrived."

"They gave us a submarine because they wanted to see where we would go with it?" Lafayette said. Then growled out a frustrated sound. "Of course they did. And now they know where the scout ship is without ever having to bother hunting for it themselves."

"And this was all Margo's work?" Tristan asked.

"More likely work done at her direction," Dieter put in. "It sounds a little outside her skill set."

"I don't know," Tristan said. "Just think about how much we've been learning just in the last few days."

"We've been learning, she and her people have been destroying things before they could learn anything," Dieter said.

"Not this, though," Tristan said. "They've kept all this for some reason. Maybe they'll do the same with the scout ship."

Dieter slumped back into the captain's chair with a heavy frown. Apparently he didn't like pondering the why of that at all.

Lafayette was willing to set it aside to ponder later, though. She finally touched the main screen of the communications console. It was far more sophisticated than the one she had used on the sunken ship. It was, in fact, an exact copy of the one she had spent so much time studying on the bridge of the ship when they were trapped under the ice.

"How can we tell a real message from a tattletale program?" Dieter asked.

"Oh, there must be a way," Kora said. "I've read

of such things, anyway. People who could disable those sorts of things."

She was waffling vaguely, Lafayette could tell. But Dieter just said, dry as ever, "From novels, I assume?"

"Yes. From novels," Kora agreed. Her teacher self had been a voracious reader, and had acquired a vast ocean of knowledge to go with her prodigious reading.

The problem was she had preferred fiction to nonfiction. And while the fiction she had consumed had been based on fact, it was hard to tell when the authors had taken liberties. But mostly, she knew things existed without knowing why or how they worked.

"We'll just have to risk it," Tristan said to Lafayette. He was hovering close over her shoulder, and she slid over on the station chair to let him share the seat with her. He took it gratefully. With their legs pressed together, she could feel how both of them were still getting muscle twitches after the long stair descent.

And they still had to get back up to the top when this was all over.

"Let's agree something looks right before either of us presses anything, all right?" she asked him.

He nodded, and they both leaned in close to examine the data on the main screen.

"That's my message," she said. She had the address and timestamp numbers memorized by now.

Then she tapped over to the messages received screen and saw at the top a message from the ship up in orbit.

"Kora, I don't think this timestamp is the same as the other," she said. Actually, she was positive it was different. But having Kora double-check her assessment just made sense.

Kora hovered up on her disk and read over Lafayette's shoulder. "You're right," she said. "This one came back almost immediately after the one you sent."

"Too soon to be a targeted program," Dieter guessed.

"There might be a way to trick the program into putting the wrong times on things," Kora warned. "But I wouldn't know how to find out, really."

"Well, like I said," Tristan said to Lafayette, "I think we just have to risk it."

Lafayette nodded, chewing at her lip. She reached out a single fingertip, but before she could quite tap the button for the playback, Tristan was seizing her hand and squeezing it with great force.

"What?" she asked. Because as much as he was

practically vibrating with excitement, he hadn't yet said anything. His eyes were just on the queue of received messages.

"Don't you see?" he said breathlessly. "There are so many responses."

"Incoming messages," Lafayette agreed.

"No, *responses*," Tristan insisted.

Dieter got up from the captain's chair to lean over Lafayette's other shoulder.

"He's right," Dieter said. "Look at that. They're flagged as replies to your message specifically."

"More programmed traps," Lafayette said with a nervous sigh. They were only assuming the first one was genuine. What if they were all traps?

"No, Lafayette," Tristan said, squeezing her hand again. He had never let it go. "Those messages…"

But he broke off with a shake of his head, then switched to another menu on the screen. Now all the messages received were charted on a three-dimensional space.

"I still don't get it," Lafayette admitted. "I've been asleep for the better part of four days. I'm not sure I'm really awake now."

"They're from space," Dieter said to her with a playful punch on her shoulder. "Like, really far away in space."

"They're right, Lafayette," Kora said. "Those

aren't part of this fleet. They're parts of other fleets. All the way back across the flight path we were following. Maybe all the way back to Earth."

"Back to..." Lafayette repeated, but trailed off. "Ugh! This makes it worse!" she all but shrieked in frustration.

"What do you mean?" Tristan asked.

"It doesn't matter if any of these messages are trapped or not, right? Because as soon as I start opening them up, Central Planning will know. And we don't know enough to find a way to stop that."

"She's right," Dieter said. "I can watch on the screen, and we can wait until they're a couple of levels away to make our escape. But they will know, and the amount of time we have at this console before they get here is minimal."

"And we need to focus on your dad, I get it," Tristan said. "But this is still good, right? To know the rest of the universe knows we're here."

"It is good," Lafayette admitted.

"Okay, play his message," Tristan said.

Lafayette reached out again. Her entire body was clenched tight in defense against any possible second round of chaotic sound.

But when she finally tapped the button, all that came out of the speakers was her father's warm voice.

"Lafayette! How wonderful to hear your voice, and I hope somehow you find a way to hear mine."

Lafayette thrust her fists up in the air in silent triumph.

"Frank Paine found a working remote station for me a few days ago, small enough to fit through the drawer here."

Which meant he was still trapped in the brig. Lafayette's hands dropped down to her lap.

"I've been using it to learn more about the systems here. Getting out of this particular room might remain beyond me for some time yet. But what can I say? It was meant to hold people with far greater technical skills than I have."

Dieter bit back a laugh at that, then stepped away from Lafayette to turn his attention to the main screen. She didn't look back at him, but she sensed his body tense up at what he saw.

So they were on their way down the stairs already. She didn't have much time.

"Look, Paine has been telling me how these communications systems work, and I know that Central Planning can trace you every time you send or receive anything. They have a high level of access, too high for even Paine to circumvent. Lafayette, it isn't safe for you. I'm well out of their reach now, but you're not. And I need you to stay safe."

Lafayette found herself nodding along to his voice in the way she always did when she was a kid. He had been the parent who was seldom there, and those nods had always been a way to placate him until he was gone again. Then she would do whatever she was going to do.

And she was doing it now. Letting his words wash over her with polite acknowledgement. But in the end, she was going to do what she was going to do.

"I've been talking with Paine, Lafayette, and we both agree the ship in the ice is the only one that's capable of getting back up here. If it falls into Central Planning hands, then I really am stuck up here. I don't know if these words will reach you in time for you to do anything, but that remains a fact."

Tristan made a frustrated sound of his own, but said nothing.

"Lafayette, I would love more than anything to see you again. I'd love to get out of this box. But I don't want you to risk your own safety to do it. It isn't what your mother would want. It isn't what I want. You need to look after yourself now. Well, you have Kora, but mostly you have you. You need to look after you. For me."

There was a long silence then, and Lafayette checked the comms screen to make sure the message was still playing. But the counter was running. Her father was just sitting in silence.

A silence he only broke at the very end of the playback to choke out the words, "Stay safe, Lafayette. I love you."

Then the message cut off.

"I don't know what I can possibly say to answer all that," Lafayette said.

"Nothing," Dieter said. "There's nothing to say until we know a way to get to him, right? Anything else is just going to hand him more worry."

"He'll know you got this," Tristan said. "He will get a notification, message received. He'll know you're still free. That's something."

"Not enough," Lafayette said, and dragged a hand across her damp cheeks. "We need to run?"

"Not the way we came," Dieter said. "Central Planning is coming down all four of the stairwells."

"There are four stairwells?" Tristan said.

But Dieter just waved the words away. "I have another path back. But I have to warn you, it's not going to be great."

"How could it be worse than those stairs in socked feet?" Lafayette asked.

Dieter licked his lips then grinned maniacally at them both.

"It's an access ladder."

CHAPTER 14

Dieter led the way out of the bridge through a smaller side corridor that ran past a dozen closed doors before ending abruptly against a thicker metal wall. If they were inside a spaceship, Lafayette would assume this wall was part of the hull and not an interior wall. She supposed in this inverted building, this wall meant they had reached the edge of the basement levels. Beyond this wall would be bedrock.

But Dieter didn't turn back. He walked right up to the blank wall and placed his palm against it. He waited a few seconds, then gave it a gentle push. Lafayette heard something inside the metal panel click, and when Dieter retracted his hand, a small doorway opened up.

This was a square set in the center of the wall panel, so Lafayette had to both duck her head low and also step over a knee-high threshold to get into the dark space on the other side of the wall.

"Go up," Dieter told her, even as he gave a floating Kora a little nudge to follow Lafayette inside.

Lafayette couldn't see a thing, but the minute she lifted her hands to feel around the space, she found the metal bars of the ladder railings. It had steps, wider than mere rungs. But they were the same expanded metal as the steps in the stairwells. And they had the same upthrusting spikes for traction that were just torture on bare feet.

Kora was already hovering her way up the space beside the ladder, so Lafayette had no choice. She started climbing after her.

At least she heard Tristan's low groan of dismay before he started up after her. She wasn't alone in her torment.

"Kora, stop when we're five levels up," Dieter hissed up the shaft, a strangely carrying whisper of sound. Then Lafayette heard the click of the panel closing behind him. The wall on the other side was once more completely featureless. Unless the Central Planning naval guards knew as much as Dieter did about this space, they would have no clue where the four of them had gone.

Lafayette caught up to where Kora was hovering and waiting. Kora had turned her indicator lights up to their maximum brightness, and the soft green light was more than enough for Lafayette to find the inside of the panel. On this side it had a handle like a drawer pull. Lafayette reversed what she had watched Dieter doing below by pulling gently on the handle and holding still for a three count, then giving it a quick jerk.

It swung open easily, and Kora floated into the red-lit corridor beyond.

Lafayette had a slightly harder time of it, shifting from the ladder built against the opposite wall through the open doorway to step down on the floor half a meter down from the bottom of the threshold. But she was careful with maintaining her handholds and managed the motion easily enough. Then she turned to help the less agile Tristan make the same transition.

"What now?" Tristan whispered the minute Dieter had joined them. Dieter didn't answer at once. First he closed the access panel behind them, then he ran his fingers over the edges as if to be absolutely sure it was flush and invisible now. At last he waved for the others to follow him.

"I found the layout of all the levels on one of the consoles on the bridge the other night," he told them. "I had to pick the important parts to memorize; forty levels of details were a little too much to swallow all at once."

"What's on this level, then?" Lafayette asked.

"Mostly, it's an opportunity to hide for a moment and let all of those guards get to the bottom," Dieter said.

"And out of the stairwells?" Tristan guessed.

"For a moment," Dieter said. "But when they don't find us at the bottom, they'll start working their way back up."

"And they'll call in other guards from the top to start working their way down," Lafayette said.

"Almost certainly," Dieter agreed. "We're only stopping here for a moment, to get off the ladder."

"You think they'll find that access tunnel?" Tristan asked.

"Well, even if they didn't, we can't climb forty levels of ladder all in one blow," Lafayette said.

Dieter just spread out his hands as if to say, "Exactly."

Then he waved for them to continue following him.

"That access hatch was the one closest to the bridge. That's why we took it first," Dieter said. "But the one I want us to end up on is on the other side of the building."

"You want us to come up directly under the operating prison?" Tristan said.

Lafayette had to be impressed by that. As much as she had no idea where the operating prison was, not having seen it herself, she still couldn't believe after all the maze-running Dieter had been having them do since breaking them out of their cells that Tristan had maintained that accurate of a mental map. He even apparently knew which direction they were facing even though they were far underground.

But Dieter just gave him a thumbs-up without slowing his rapid pace through the grid of corridors they were traversing. At every crossing of corridors, he would either take them straight, or he would turn left for one block of rooms, then turn right so they were heading straight on again.

"Anything of use in any of these rooms?" Lafayette asked. The doors were all closed, but she couldn't help remembering the closet they had been hiding in first. The shelves had been entirely bare. There hadn't even been any dust on the floor.

"No, they stripped everything before they tore the ship apart," Dieter said. "There are some spaces labeled as storerooms, but they are on the top of the sub-basements. Directly under the prison itself."

"So we have to climb thirty-something more levels in socks," Tristan said.

"Hey," Dieter said with a grin. "At least we're not in danger of freezing to death."

"There's always that," Lafayette agreed.

They had reached the deadend of another corridor against a hull-like wall. Dieter gestured for silence before gently opening the hatchway, then slowly putting his head inside. Lafayette watched as he looked first down, then up, before finally stepping inside to lead the way up the ladder.

Kora hovered after him, then Lafayette helped Tristan make the reach from corridor floor to ladder rungs. He was clearly nervous, clinging so tightly to the doorframe that his knuckles were visibly white even in the dim red glow of the emergency lights. But he made the step across easily enough and started after Dieter.

Lafayette stepped out onto the ladder, carefully closed the panel behind her and made sure it was secure, then tried not to flinch too much as she followed the others.

It was just, those spiky bits of the expanded metal were in the same place on every rung. So they kept digging into the same spots on the bottoms of her feet over and over. It was torture.

Dieter climbed about ten levels this time before opening another hatch into a corridor.

"Just to rest?" Tristan was asking when Lafayette emerged behind him into the corridor. She could tell he was trying not to sound like he needed a break already. But she was pretty sure he needed a break.

"I think we're both high enough above the bottom and low enough from the top to try using the stairs for a bit," Dieter said. "If we see any light at all, we have to get out of the stairwell at once. The odds of them seeing us across big distances are low, but they're not zero. Not with all the gaps in the expanded metal on the stairs."

"Sure," Tristan agreed. "We move fast, silent, and on high alert."

Dieter just nodded, then led them to the nearest stairwell. The physical structure of the stairs was identical to the stairwell they had used before, but the rock around it was different. It looked more metamorphic than igneous to Lafayette's eyes, but that wasn't saying much. Granted, she knew enough about geology to make that fairly rudimentary distinction. But the light was low, and she didn't exactly dare pause even for a momentary closer inspection. She just had a vague sense of more layering lines, fewer glints of crystalline structures buried in the rock here than at the other side of the building.

At first, Lafayette thought that Dieter was setting too slow a pace, erring too much on the side of caution, perhaps. But after going up about a dozen levels, and knowing that meant they were only about halfway up, she could see the sense in his pacing choice. It was steady, relentless. But it was just barely manageable.

For her. She supposed Tristan was having a tougher time.

But when she glanced up to check on him, he seemed to be doing okay. He had come a long way since they had met, and especially since that day they had criss-crossed all the capital city after going up and down the shaft of the hidden space-ship at the heart of the city. He had found reserves of stamina he hadn't even known he had.

Lafayette lost count of the levels, but she was pretty sure they had less than ten left to go when Dieter abruptly veered off, plastering himself against the side of the metal wall dividing the stairwell from the rest of the basement structure. Without a word between them, Tristan and La-fayette copied this move. Even Kora pressed her hovering body close to the wall.

Then she heard it: the sound of footsteps coming from somewhere up above them. She craned her neck, but there was no hint of a light or any kind of motion. But she knew what she had heard.

And Dieter had heard it too. She watched as he crept to the nearest door, eased it open with agonizing slowness, then held it just wide enough for Kora to float past him into the corridor beyond.

Tristan crept up next, turning sideways to slide through the doorway. Lafayette followed, freezing mid-step for half a second when another crunch of a boot on a landing above her echoed down. It was closer, for sure, but not too close. Yet.

She ducked into the corridor, and Dieter whisked in right after her with the grace of a dancer. He eased the door shut again, then motioned for them all to run.

He had to take the lead again, since he had the best sense of where they were going. Although Tristan hadn't looked lost even when Dieter sprinted past him, then took a sharp turn to the left.

Lafayette looked back over her shoulder, almost wishing she had stayed closer to the door. If it opened up, she would know they were about to be caught. But short of that, she was too far away to hear anything. If whoever was in the stairwell carried on down to the lower levels, making them safe for the time being, they wouldn't even know.

She'd prefer to know. But she couldn't risk getting separated from the others.

She turned her head to face front again and picked up her pace, sprinting almost soundlessly around the turn to the left and just reaching the end of the corridor as Tristan disappeared through the access hatch to the ladder beyond.

Lafayette climbed inside but hesitated with the door still open, straining her ears to hear anything save the sounds of her friends climbing the rungs above her.

Then she heard it. A soft click. Someone was on this level. The click had echoed oddly through the empty corridors, like it could've come from anywhere. Like, not necessarily that stairwell. Like, possibly somewhere much, much closer.

Lafayette held her breath as she closed the hatch behind her and made double sure it was properly sealed.

Then she hustled up the ladder to catch up with the others.

Dieter led them up past the top levels of the sub-basements, to a point where their squared-off access space became a less sophisticatedly manufactured tunnel through pure stone. When they left the last of the metal interior walls behind them and were completely enclosed in stone, the ladder changed as well. The steps with their nubs were now gone, replaced by rusted rings of irregularly manufactured iron.

They had to slow down just to be sure of each step now. And Lafayette knew she wasn't the only one trying not to think about how very long the fall back down was.

Of course the others had an added wrinkle of having friends below them. If she fell, she'd hurt no one but herself.

If either of them fell… well, Lafayette didn't like the odds of her being strong enough to stop them, no matter how narrow the space was.

Her bleak thoughts were dispelled in an instant when a shaft of warm light struck her face. Sunlight. It was sunlight. She hadn't felt the touch of the sun in days.

And she could hear birds again. The sound of seabirds squabbling over scraps. It was so close.

But all she could see when she looked up was the dirty soles of Tristan's socks. Or what remained of his socks. Although she doubted hers looked much better.

Then Dieter and Tristan both reached down for her, helping her out of a round metal hatch and onto a coarse stone floor. She wanted nothing more than to flop down on the ground and rest for a thousand years. But when she did no more than put a knee down on that stone, Dieter and Tristan both started hissing almost silent objections at her. They were waving their hands frantically, and she took the hint enough to stay on her two feet.

Then she looked around and saw where they

were. In the prison section, clearly. They were standing at the top of a stone tower that overlooked most of the island compound, and she could see the fabricated metal of the naval installation off to the west.

There were other stone guard towers on this eastern side of the compound, and she could see dots of people inside. Which explained why Dieter was hunched over so that his head wasn't much higher than the parapet that boxed them in. Tristan, being significantly shorter, just had to duck his head a little to stay out of sight.

Then she finally saw why the other two hadn't wanted to touch the ground here. It was covered in layer upon layer of bird excrement. The parapet itself was littered with nests, some that looked like their occupants were only temporarily away, but others that looked like they'd been abandoned for years.

That would explain why there were no human guards up in this particular tower. Or, perhaps, the lack of humans explained the proliferation of birds here. Certainly, it was an ideal roosting spot. To the east there was nothing but the sheer side of the stone wall of the compound, then the nearly equally steep side of a natural cliff that ended in a narrow strip of beach far below.

A beach dotted with little furry animals that

looked like brown commas from all the way up here.

But those commas were definitely the source of the barking sounds she'd been hearing for days. Whatever those furry little creatures were, they frolicked together like puppies in the sand and in the rolling surf.

"This is a perfect vantage point," Tristan said. "With the sun rising behind us, no one can see us up here. At least not easily. But look, there's the submarine fleet in the harbor over there. And there's your airship on the landing field. Any arriving ship with Margo on board will surely land there too. And that's the prison yard where they exercise the prisoners."

"We can certainly keep a watch from here," Dieter said. "But we're going to have to find some place just a little cleaner for sleeping and eating."

"Not to mention something to eat. And water would be nice," Lafayette said.

"Give me a minute," Dieter said.

Then he disappeared back down the ladder they had just emerged from.

CHAPTER 15

Despite the chill in the breeze blowing in off the ocean, Lafayette took off her button-up shirt, leaving her only in her sleeveless tank top. Then she tore two long strips off the bottom of her shirt and handed one to Tristan.

"What's this?" he asked, distracted from his gazing over the parapet.

"Put it over your nose and mouth," Lafayette told him, even as she tied her own around her head just under her hair puffs. "All of this bird poop is more than gross; it's a biological hazard. We're not in an enclosed space here, which is good, but we're surrounded by dried bird droppings turning into dust, and that's absolutely not good."

"Oh, right," Tristan said, then tied his own face mask on. Lafayette couldn't help grinning under her own mask. He looked just like a bandit now, ready to rustle up out of the cover of the grasslands and rob a trading caravan. One from the stories she had grown up on as a kid. But she supposed she did, too.

"Where is the prison exercise yard?" Lafayette asked, creeping slowly to stand closer to the parapet without touching it. At all. It was so nasty.

But also, she wasn't as confident as Tristan that no one could see them up here. The other guard towers were all quite a bit lower than the one they were in now, and no one seemed to be looking their way. But that could change in a hurry.

"Over there, by the airfield," Tristan said, pointing off to the north. There was a field of packed dirt, broken up here and there by the hardier of the local weeds, between the wall of the prison building and the outer wall beyond. There were more guard towers atop that outer wall, but like the one they were standing in now, they appeared long abandoned to anything but bird occupation.

"And you saw prisoners out there when we were refueling?" Lafayette asked.

"Yes, they were walking in a line, going in a circle over and over and not really looking up," he said. "I didn't see Uche."

Lafayette just nodded. He had told her that before. She closed her eyes and tried to reach out with all her senses. Did she *feel* like Uche was here on this island with her?

Not that she thought her heart had such powers. But her brain noticed things subconsciously sometimes, and it needed a little quiet introspection to bring it out to her conscious mind. So she did that now. She let her mind go still like a pond and waited to see if anything would rise to the surface. Did she have any reason to think that Uche was there?

But she just didn't know. She wanted to hope he was. She longed to have him that close.

But hope could be such a trap. Particularly in a situation like this one, where the thing that made the most sense was for the four of them to continue running, as far and for as long as they could.

"The airship is in good condition," Tristan noted. "But clearly under guard. It would be tricky to get to it."

"Easier than getting to any of the submarines or boats," Lafayette said. The docks around the harbor were heavily patrolled on foot and with small watercraft. Sneaking through that area would be all but impossible.

"Maybe at night, with some kind of diversion, we could steal that airship again," Tristan said.

"We kind of have to," Lafayette said.

"All of our stuff is on there?" he said, clearly trying for a lighthearted joke. He was just as worried about their journals as she was, she knew.

But Lafayette was worried about more than losing all their work. "Kora's paste," she said.

"Oh," Tristan said, his face behind the mask clearly falling. "Yeah, right. We need that. As soon as we can get it."

"I can function for a few more days," Kora told them both brightly.

Then they all turned at the sound of the hatch swinging open behind them once more. Dieter climbed out, did a double-take at their masked faces, then broke into a grin.

"Smart. But I found something more suitable. Follow me."

Lafayette tried not to sigh too loudly, but getting back on a ladder was just about the last thing she wanted to be doing just then.

Luckily, Dieter didn't take them far. They came down the stone tunnel to the top of the last stairwell, then ducked into the top-level sub-basement door. But he only led them a few meters down a hallway before doing his little trick in the middle of the corridor to open another hidden hatch in the exterior wall.

It wasn't a vertical access channel with a ladder this time, but a horizontal channel of about the same tight dimensions. Too low to walk through for any of them save Kora, they all crawled on their hands and knees for a dozen or so meters.

Then Dieter disappeared, dropping down from the end of the horizontal shaft to some open space below. Tristan dropped down after him, followed by the floating Kora. Then Lafayette slid down after them.

They were in a stone-walled space, a decent enough square room about the size of their airship gondola but far taller. Lafayette looked up, but all she could see was shaft opening after shaft opening, all ending in this space.

"Is this going to fill up with water or something?" Lafayette asked. Because everything lately felt like another possible trap.

"No, this is where the ventilation system for the sub-basements meets the ventilation system for the prison itself," Dieter said. "It's a very bad design, even given the circumstances."

"What circumstances?" Tristan asked. He was

examining the stone floor beneath their socked feet. There were a few dried tropical leaves and a bit of dust, but nothing too problematic. He pulled down his face mask and left it hanging around his neck.

"The information I had about the sub-basements included the building timeline from back in the day," Dieter said. "This prison has been here for a hundred years or so, right?"

"If you say so," Tristan said with a shrug.

"Right, so that's how old this technology is," Dieter said, pointing at the shafts above them. "But then these sub-basements were tunneled out only in the last decade."

"So it's newer," Lafayette said.

"Well, that's just the thing," Dieter said. "They filled it with what they scavenged from the spaceship they found out here. And those parts are older. Far older."

"And yet more technologically advanced," Tristan said, nodding. "At least compared to what Central Planning lets the rest of us have."

"Right," Dieter agreed.

"They built this a decade ago, but they're only just now starting to use it?" Lafayette asked.

"I think they initially only wanted to hide the spaceship where no one else would find it, and this was the best way they could think of to do that," Dieter said. "The sheer dimensions of the volume of a full wheel with spokes… there'd be nowhere to hide a hangar big enough to contain it. But when you dismantle it and reassemble it in the tightest configuration possible—"

"You end up with a forty-story building that goes straight down instead of straight up," Tristan said. "I don't know if I'd build that on an island, though."

"The ship came down near here," Lafayette said. "They had to hide it near here. They couldn't move it, not even piece by piece. Too many pieces."

"I wish this was closer to that tower," Tristan said. "Going through the stairwell is going to be risky."

"Yeah, I don't think we should attempt it again, as nice as that vantage point was," Dieter said. "But give me a little time. I haven't been through the ventilation system in the prison proper yet. I'll start exploring and see what I can find."

"Now?" Lafayette asked.

"Well, I was going to nap first," he admitted with a dry grin.

"We do have a ticking clock," Lafayette said, trying to point at Kora without Kora noticing.

"A couple of ticking clocks, really," Tristan added.

"I know," Dieter said. "Look, I don't want to get anyone else's hopes up, but I should probably tell you all there's a remote possibility that my family is on their way here."

"Really?" Lafayette asked, clearly with too much enthusiasm to judge from Dieter's wince.

"Remote! Very remote," he said, waving his hands in a calm-down gesture.

"How?" Tristan asked.

"When Lafayette sent the message to us to run, I forwarded it on," Dieter said. "All channels, maximum signal boost. It went out to all ships. I mean, given the nature of the message, there was no longer any point in secrecy, right?"

"And your family got it?" Lafayette asked.

"Well, that's the thing," he said. "I boosted it enough to carry around the world, or pretty close to it. But Central Planning started broadcasting this wall of static right after."

"Oh!" Tristan said with a flush to his cheeks. "I heard that. The double play of Lafayette's message, then the shriek of loud static. I thought the submarine's communications equipment was just fried. I mean, I hadn't tested it or used it or anything."

"No, they have a way of blocking anyone else from using their channels, I guess," Dieter said. "At any rate, if my family sent any response, I never got it. And those airships that ran me down showed up so soon afterwards."

"They were waiting," Lafayette said. "They were watching and waiting. And I fell right into their trap."

"You fell into someone's trap," Dieter said. "But I think it might be a mistake to think *of Central* Planning as one big entity wi*th one common goal."*

"What do you mean?" Tristan asked.

"I've been pondering it for quite some time. It's the only way I can make Margo and what she's doing against the background of all the rest of Central Planning we've been running up against make sense," Dieter said. "Someone on the inside is… I don't know. Playing a political game."

"Margo?" Lafayette said. Because that didn't seem likely.

And indeed Dieter was already shaking his head. "If anything, I think someone is using Margo. Kind of like how they're using us."

"Using us to find things. Because they aren't supposed to be looking for these things," Tristan said musingly. "No one is supposed to go out and find anything to do with our ancestors. No one should be doing anything that contributes to more proof that we're not really from this planet. That we come from somewhere else."

"So they ban history and they ban archaeology," Lafayette grumbled. "They target my parents and teachers like Uche Okafo. And they burn books."

"But someone clearly still wants the technology," Dieter said. "But it's not someone who can just go get it. They can get their hands on it if it's in the name of protecting the people. But they can't go looking for it."

"They sank the ship in the north," Lafayette said.

"But they didn't destroy it," Dieter said. "They just… set it aside. Somewhere safe until they can get to it later."

"Who?" Lafayette asked.

"Someone up on that tall tower in the middle of the capital," Tristan said glumly. "The one they never come down from."

"So, what do we do now?" Lafayette asked.

"Now? We sleep," Dieter said, even as he settled with his back against the wall in what looked like one of the cleaner bits of floor. "I just need a few hours. Then I'll find food and water for us all."

"And shoes?" Lafayette asked.

"Might be trickier, but the prisoners are wearing them so they must have stores somewhere," Dieter said, already closing his eyes and folding his arms over his chest.

Lafayette settled with her back against the opposite wall, and Kora moved over to lie down beside her.

Then Tristan sat down on her other side, gesturing for her to lean up against him. He put his arm around her, draping the folds of his shirt around her as much as he could.

She hadn't even realized she was rubbing her arms from the cold. But he had seen it.

"We'll resupply tomorrow," he said. "In the meantime, I really don't think anyone is going to find us in here. Do you?"

"I'll keep watch," Kora said primly before Lafayette could say anything at all.

"Appreciate that," Dieter said to her, not opening his eyes. But his tone heavily implied that it was quiet time now.

Lafayette looked up into Tristan's face and mouthed the words "good night" to him, silently. He returned the gesture. Then they snuggled in tighter with Kora sprawled across both their laps and tried to catch what sleep they could.

CHAPTER 16

afayette never heard when Dieter woke up and slipped out of their little room, and apparently Tristan hadn't either. But they both snapped awake when he landed with a thump in front of them, his arms loaded with three stuffed rucksacks.

"How long were you gone?" Tristan asked sleepily.

"A bit," Dieter said. "Kora was keeping watch. You guys were fine."

"I mean, we could've helped," Lafayette said.

"Get dressed," Dieter said, shoving one of the rucksacks at her. "We're moving house."

Lafayette opened the top of the rucksack and

saw several pairs of khaki pants with matching loose-fitting shirts that tied in the front.

Tristan took one of those shirts out of his own sack and held it up before saying to Dieter, "Prison uniforms?"

"It will help us blend in," Dieter said.

"As prisoners," Lafayette said. "Isn't that a little risky?"

"Isn't all of this?" Dieter countered. "Now you've got clean clothes and shoes, and I've found us a better hidey-hole. We won't have to pass as prisoners if no one sees us, and Plan A is still no one seeing us."

They all turned their backs on each other and got out of their dirty—and in Lafayette's case torn—clothes and into the surprisingly comfortable prison uniforms. The uniforms even came with matching hats, just soft cloth things that were just large enough to cover their ears, designed to keep the sun off more than for warmth.

This was clearly not a work camp; these clothes were far too lightweight to stand up to that. Lafayette doubted they could even stand up to be sweated in for long. They were practically tissue paper was it was. Which was probably why Dieter had brought so many changes of clothes for each of them.

And extra pairs of shoes. Because the prison

shoes were little more than slippers with very thin bottoms. They weren't going to hold up much better than the socks had if they had to do more stair running today.

Still, when she had tied up her shirt and slipped on her shoes, she turned back to Dieter to ask, "How long do you think we'll be hiding here on the island?"

"We can make a try for the airship at any time," Dieter said. "But we should aim for before Margo gets here. On the other hand, I'd love to give my family a chance to get here. Their numbers are going to increase our odds of getting out of here alive. And, I assume, you want a chance to be sure whether Uche is being held here or not."

"Can we see the prison from our new hiding place?" Tristan asked as he closed up his sack and slung it over his shoulder.

"Oh yes," Dieter said with a grin. "I found us a room like this, but with a grill that looks out over the prison yard. We can watch all day and all night from there."

"Lead the way," Lafayette said.

Dieter slung his own sack onto his back, then jumped up to catch the lip of the lowest shaft. He then pulled himself past it, to the next shaft opening. And then a third time, hanging practically by his fingertips before hoisting himself into an opening that was a good ten meters up.

"Um, Diet?" Tristan called up nervously.

"I got you, Trist," Dieter said as he tossed down a rope.

"I'll go up first," Lafayette volunteered. "Maybe you'll want to tie your sack to the end of the rope? Then we can pull it up after you're done climbing."

"Yeah, sure," Tristan agreed, shifting his weight from foot to foot in a show of nerves.

Lafayette scaled the rope easily enough, then turned to see Tristan already halfway up behind her. He really was getting stronger.

"Are we good influences or bad influences?" Dieter asked her, apparently seeing the same changes in Tristan as she did.

"I think we're a mixed bag," Lafayette decided.

Dieter chuckled to himself, then leaned out of the shaft opening to catch the back of Tristan's pants and help him get over the lip. Not that he needed it.

Kora, floating as gently as ever, brought up the rear. Then they hauled in the rope, and Tristan settled his pack on his shoulders.

This shaft was no bigger than the other, which meant more crawling on hands and feet. No one was talking, but at one point Dieter turned back to look at Lafayette and Tristan trailing behind him. He put a finger to his lips and saw their nods before he continued on.

The shaft looked the same as ever, and Dieter made no sound crawling ahead. But Lafayette knew in an instant why he had signaled for them to be extra quiet. There was the smallest of creaks as she crawled, and she knew that what was on the other side of the metal under her hands now wasn't stone. It was open air.

The air shaft they were crawling through was running along a ceiling, passing over an open space. And it was one occupied by people. Lafayette heard a murmuring of voices down below her. She couldn't catch any words, but it sounded like idle chatter, like people talking softly over a meal or something similar. It was a lot of people, though. Her mind conjured the mental image of a cafeteria.

But the echos were funny. So she adjusted her image. A cafeteria built to feed hundreds, now holding only a few dozen. That felt right.

Then they were past that point, and once more following a channel built into the stone wall.

They reached a crossroads, but Dieter kept on ahead. Then, all at once, he dropped out of sight ahead of her. There was a quality to the light like sunlight, but she couldn't see where it was coming from.

Then she reached the drop-off herself and slid her feet around to the front before dropping down to where Dieter was waiting for her on the ground below. It was a long but narrow space, barely wide enough to walk down single file, so La- fayette had to be sure to land behind Dieter and not on top of him. Then she ducked under his armpit to slip past him, leaving room for Tristan to land where she had just been.

"What is this?" Tristan asked in a low whisper. It wasn't exactly a corridor, as there were no doors and it was so excessively narrow. There were a few other air shafts at various heights, but all on the side they had just dropped down from. But mostly there were pipes and bundles of wires run- ning in both directions along the channel.

Then Lafayette tipped her head back and saw where the sunlight was coming from. There was a tiled roof far overhead, broken up here and there by extremely grimy windows.

"Utility access," Dieter said, keeping his voice low but not exactly whispering. "There are a few doors in from the prison, but they're all locked. Doors and locks both are beyond rusty. I think it's safe to say no one ever comes in here."

"But they could. If they wanted to," Tristan said.

"We won't give them a reason to," Dieter said. "Come on. The space where we're going to set up camp is just a little further along."

He took Lafayette by the shoulders and got her moving in the direction she was facing. He followed along behind her, then Tristan, and Kora—on her feet now that floating was no longer necessary—brought up the rear.

They walked for several minutes before Dieter stopped Lafayette's motion with a hand on her shoulder. Only then did she see the ladder built into the wall on her right. They only had to go up a couple of meters, though. She clambered up it, then had to crawl forward. She wasn't in a ventilation shaft this time, more like this particular loft space had been built with very little room around the central beam that supported the tile ceiling. It was a little claustrophobic, but only for a minute.

Then she was on the other side of the beam and could straighten up. She had been right; it was a loft. There were more skylights here, although they were just as grimy as the others.

But there was also a grill at the very end of the space, tucked close beside the beam. Lafayette dropped her rucksack on the wood planks of the loft floor, then crept forward to peer out of that grill.

She did, indeed, have a bird's-eye view of the exercise yard from here. It was currently empty, but it was barely past breakfast time yet. The grill was about ten meters off the ground, plenty high enough to make noticing anyone looking out of it a little unlikely.

"Nice space," Tristan said as he, too, dropped his rucksack on the ground. But he was noticing something on the other side of the room that Lafayette had missed.

A sink. A sink that, when Tristan turned the spigot, actually worked. It poured sparkling water into a wide, square basin set into the floor. Rather like the bottom of a shower stall, only with no walls and no shower head, just a faucet set at mid-calf height.

"There's food in the packs under the clothes," Dieter told them both. "No bedrolls, but I did find blankets. Except for Kora's paste, I think we have everything we need, at least for a few days."

"We can't stay here longer than that," Lafayette said.

"Agreed," Dieter said.

"We can't see the airfield from here," Tristan said, leaning over Lafayette's shoulder to catch the view of the yard briefly before straightening up again.

"We *can*," Dieter hedged. Then he pointed to yet another ladder, this one running beside the beam up to the very top of the roof. There was a hatch there, currently closed. "You can see most of the prison side of the compound from there. But it's very exposed. I only took a glance through it last night, and that was under the cover of darkness. We can risk it at night, maybe. If we're very brief and very, very careful."

"This is perfect," Lafayette said, settling in to spend as much time as possible gazing through the ventilation grill.

She wasn't going anywhere until she caught sight of Uche. Or every other prisoner in the place, she supposed. Just to be sure he wasn't here.

"I'm catching another nap," Dieter announced, digging a blanket out of his rucksack. "I have a feeling the middle of the day is going to get a little steamy in here, but it can't be helped. Once it's dark again, I'll head out for a little more recon."

"Can't we help?" Tristan asked.

"It's safer if it's just me," Dieter said.

Tristan nodded his acknowledgement of this. But Lafayette could tell he didn't like it. She couldn't blame him. She didn't like feeling useless either. And waiting around was maddening. Especially knowing all the work that waited for them once they got back to the airship and all their journals.

"Do you want to trade shifts with me, watching for Uche?" Lafayette asked. "It'll break up the standing a little."

"Absolutely," Tristan said.

Kora padded around the loft several times, smelling this corner and that, but never speaking to any of them. Finally she flung herself down by Dieter's side and let her own eyes close.

"Is she doing okay?" Tristan asked, barely louder than a breath.

"She's conserving her energy, I think," Lafayette said.

Although it was worrying, how little Kora was talking. Because if there was one thing she didn't need any of her biological dog energy to do, it was talking. That was fueled entirely by the battery in her robotic abdomen.

It was probably just the feeling of confinement, Lafayette decided. Because as much as they had escaped their captors, they hadn't exactly escaped their captivity.

And it was anybody's guess when they'd be able to do that.

CHAPTER 17

Lafayette and Tristan spent the next three days entirely inside that loft, taking turns watching through the ventilation grill as prison life played out before them.

They had yet to see Uche, which was frustrating. They could prove he was there by seeing him. But not seeing him didn't quite prove that he wasn't there.

But somewhere in his roaming, Dieter had found a soft white rock that worked almost like chalk. The marks it made on the stone wall were faint, but clear enough.

By the end of the first day in that loft, they had a pretty good idea of what the schedule was for exercise time and guard rotations. Or at least as much of the guard rotation as they could see from their perch by the grill.

By the end of the second day, they'd come up with nicknames for every prisoner and guard and had a list of who would be where and when.

By the end of the third day, they knew their list was solid. Everyone turned up just when they expected them to without fail. It was starting to really feel like they'd done everything they could to verify that Uche really wasn't being held on the island.

"If he were being held anywhere in the capital city, I'm sure my brothers would have busted him out by now," Dieter said. He had stolen an entire crate of applesauce in single-serving foil envelopes on one of his nighttime recon excursions and was squeezing them into his mouth one by one, leaving a pile of shining wrappers in the corner of the loft.

"I'm actually feeling really good about our chances of getting our airship back," Tristan said. "We've been watching these guards for days now. They couldn't be less interested in their jobs."

"Well," Dieter said with a drawl as he ripped open another applesauce packet. "These guards here? Yes. They are guarding prisoners who know there's nowhere for them to go even if they get out of the walls of the prison. No one is really attempting to escape from here."

"But?" Lafayette asked.

"What the more motivated guards are assigned to is the airfield and the harbor," Dieter said. "That's the only way off this island. I've watched the guards there myself. Granted, not as thoroughly as you two have charted this area's activities," he added with a wave towards the scribbles they had made all over the stone wall. "But I can tell you they are taking it seriously on the other side of the island. They are alert, and they don't let their patrolling fall into any predictable pattern. There is a lot of redundancy. I'm not saying it's impossible. I think if we're a little bit clever and a lot lucky we can do it. But it's not going to be as easy as looking out that grill might lead you to believe."

"Getting the airship free was always going to be the hardest part, I think," Lafayette said. She made a gesture, and Dieter responded by tossing her one of the applesauce packets. It was quite possibly the worst applesauce she'd ever eaten, but sucking it out of the foil packet was at least something to do to pass the time.

But something caught Tristan's attention. She saw it even before he said a word in the way his spine straightened up and he leaned ever so slightly closer to the grill.

"What is it?" Lafayette asked in a low voice.

"Something is happening. Not in the prison yard, but I think at the airfield. The guards out in the yard are all looking that way." He gestured off to his left, the direction of the airfield.

Lafayette turned to look at Dieter, but he was already moving. He tossed the sucked-dry remains of his last packet over his shoulder as he approached the ladder up to the roof. He zipped up it at record speed but then paused a moment before slowly easing the hatch open.

It was still the middle of the afternoon. Probably the very worst time to attempt this maneuver, given the way the afternoon sun would glint off of that metal hatch. He was potentially flashing a light to draw every guard's attention their way, even if he was careful.

She watched as he rose up on tiptoe on the ladder rungs, leaning a little further out of the loft without lifting the hatch any more than he had to. Then he softly set it closed again and came back down, jumping the last bunch of rungs to land in front of Lafayette.

"And?" she said.

"It's Margo Weiss. She's here," he said.

"We wanted to be gone *before* she got here," Lafayette grumbled, fisting her hands and pacing. It was all she could do to burn off frustration.

"If at all possible," Dieter said. "And it wasn't. At all possible."

"She's in uniform?" Tristan asked.

"I'm sure she had more than one," Dieter smirked at him.

"Obviously he means—" Lafayette started to say, but Dieter cut her off.

"Yes. She's still in uniform. All the guards are saluting her approach, then jumping double-time to do her bidding," Dieter said. "She still has authority."

"Sounds like more authority than I had when I wore that uniform," Tristan grumbled. Which was true. They had gotten a resupply for their airship and the use of a submarine. But what they hadn't gotten, despite the use of the mysterious red uniform, was any deference or sense of having rank.

Yeah, they totally should have suspected the whole thing was a trap. It had gone way too smoothly.

Lafayette resumed her pacing. She had been holding on to a slim hope that being mutinied by her airship crew and then losing her quarry had been enough to get Margo demoted or suspended or something. But apparently it had not.

"If it makes you feel any better, she looked furious just now," Dieter said, between sucks from another packet of applesauce. "I think they just told her they had no idea where her prisoners got off to. It's not like they tried hard to find us."

"Why would they bother?" Lafayette said. "They just had to guard the only means we had of getting off this island. Which they did quite effectively. They knew we were still here. It didn't really matter that they didn't know where specifically we were."

"They're going to do a more thorough search now," Tristan guessed. "She's not going to let them get by with any less."

"No, our time is mostly definitely up," Dieter said. "Even so, trying to get out before we have the cover of darkness will certainly be a mistake. Just a few hours and it will be sundown. Then we'll go get our airship back."

"You have a plan?" Lafayette stopped pacing to ask him.

The chagrined look on his face told her he didn't. But then Tristan sucked in a breath behind her, and she spun to see him pressing his face close to the grill again.

"It's him!" he hissed. "It's Uche! I can see him out in the yard!"

Lafayette and Dieter both crowded around Tristan's shoulders. There was no need to point him out. Despite being dressed exactly the same as everyone else, Uche stood a bit taller than all the other prisoners, and his was holding his sunhat in one hand rather than wearing it on his head.

The tall shock of his silvery-gray hair was very distinctive. He usually wore it tied back at the nape of his neck, but perhaps the prison banned any kind of binding. Or expected the prisoners to wear the hats. But without that tie, it was a lot of hair.

"What do we do?" Kora said, suddenly not only awake but excited. She was practically chasing her own tail.

"We'll get to him," Lafayette said, trading glances with Tristan.

"Yes," Tristan said thoughtfully. But then he perked up. "Yes! Look! The guards are breaking rotation. It looks like half of them are being called away."

"To look for us," Dieter said forcefully.

"But that only leaves a couple watching the prisoners," Lafayette said. "We'll never have another chance like this."

"We don't have a chance now," Dieter said. His eyes moved from Tristan to Lafayette and then back again. Then he blew out a frustrated sigh.

"We wait until they're just about to go in," he

said at last. "There's an alcove off the yard directly under this grill. If you can lure him over there, out of view of those two guard towers, then fine. But you can't go out into that field to get him. They will catch you. Hats or no hats, they have your descriptions."

"Got it," Lafayette and Tristan said as one. Then they dug through their rucksacks for the cloth hats that matched their uniforms.

"We aren't going to need any of this stuff anymore," Tristan said, frowning down at his rucksack.

"No, better to leave it all behind. We'll be faster unburdened," Dieter said.

"How do we get to this alcove?" Lafayette asked.

"There's a door at the end of the access hallway. You'll have to put a shoulder to it to get it to open. It's not rusted shut, but the dirt outside has blown up over it, and it's a little bit blocked," Dieter said.

"The door is right under us?" Tristan asked, suddenly going pale despite the afternoon heat inside the stuffy loft.

"Kora has been on high alert," Dieter said.

"Every minute," Kora said with a nod to Dieter that felt like a salute.

And Lafayette realized that answered everything she'd been worried about. Kora wasn't quiet because she was feeling low energy from being tired or lacking nutrients from her food. She was being quiet because all her senses were on high alert, and the computer brain that processed them all was always running at maximum efficiency. Just to be sure no one in the prison sneaked up on them while their own guard was down.

"Good girl," Lafayette said, which was funny. She had never felt less like she was talking to the dog she had known throughout her childhood.

But Kora didn't mind. She just swished her orange brush of a tail with all the enthusiasm in her doggy body.

"Try to get to Uche," Dieter said to Tristan and Lafayette, drawing her attention back to him. "If you can get him away from here, then bring him."

"You think he won't leave?" Lafayette asked, puzzled.

"I think he might be recovering from illness or… I don't know. Something worse. I absolutely know he won't want to slow you down," Dieter said.

Lafayette was distracted for a moment, trying to guess what Dieter was picturing when he said "something worse."

But Tristan just said, "We'll convince him. He'll come."

Dieter looked skeptical, but just shrugged, not inclined to argue.

"Where will you be?" Lafayette asked him.

"I'm going to get up a bit higher, back to that tower that the birds have taken over," he said. "I want to get one last good look around at the horizon and all."

"For your family," Lafayette guessed.

"I know they're coming. Nothing would stop them," he said, putting a fist over his heart as if swearing it as an oath. But then he faltered, as if remembering his own words that the chance was remote and not worth putting all their hopes on. He went on, "But also, I want to see the entire compound before I decide on the best route to the airship."

"So, what do we do?" Tristan asked.

"With or without Uche, I need you to stay hidden in the prison yard," Dieter said. "Once it's good and dark, I'll come find you there. You know where the guard towers are, and you know the usual rotation. You'll be fine."

"And Kora?" Lafayette asked.

Kora swished her tail again, but hesitantly this time.

Dieter didn't answer for a long time. He just looked down at the dog as the dog gazed up at Lafayette.

"I think she's safer with me," he finally said. "You two are running right towards the guards. I'm not arguing with you about it, but that *is* what you're basically doing. And there's not a prison uniform in the world that is going to make Kora look less like a dog. She's safer with me."

"I agree," Tristan said softly. "For what it's worth."

"Kora?" Lafayette said. Because no matter what her own feelings on the matter were, the decision was really Kora's to make.

Kora tipped her head to one side like she were pondering her answer. Or listening to some sound none of the three humans could hear. Then she straightened up again to look up at Lafayette.

"I think I should go with Dieter. He's going to be running over rooftops, but with my hover disks, I'll be all right. And I'm more likely to stay out of sight there," she said.

"Especially as we're not running over rooftops until after sundown," Dieter said. "We'll be in that bird tower until then."

"And we'll be just outside that door, in the alcove," Tristan said.

"Don't split up," Dieter said, pointing a commanding finger first at Lafayette and then at Tristan. "I'm serious. No matter what, you two stick together."

"I promise," Tristan said earnestly.

"Promise," Lafayette echoed.

Then they exchanged questioning looks and nods. They were both ready to go.

"Stay safe," Dieter called after them as they bent to crawl back under the beam to the access hallway.

"You too," Tristan said, then crawled out of sight.

"Kora, keep him safe," Lafayette said.

"I promise," Kora said.

And then it was her turn to leave their safe space behind.

Who knew what awaited her on the other side?

CHAPTER 18

Tristan pushed the door open, leaning his shoulder into it. The dirt on the other side had indeed drifted up on the outside, over enough time that rain and wind had hardened it into a ridge with the consistency of pottery. It finally broke away, shattering into pieces, and the two of them stepped outside.

They were standing on the edge of the exercise yard, mostly hidden from view from the guard towers by what appeared to be some sort of storage shed directly in front of them. Although what could be stored inside a structure with no apparent door or window to get inside was a bit of a mystery.

To the left, Lafayette could see past a nasty-looking wire fence to the airfield. It was the same hard-packed clay-like dirt as the exercise yard. There were two airships moored there now: the one they had stolen and used to escape from the polar ice, and a smaller, older model. That had to be what Margo had finally taken to come after them.

There were a few guards milling around the new arrival, not exactly in a patrol formation. But their airship had two burly guards standing just at the door. They had guns on their belts and riot sticks in their hands.

Lafayette adjusted her cap a little lower over her head. Any glimpse of her red-tipped hair buns and they would instantly know she wasn't really a prisoner here. Even without Kora at her side, she was too distinctive.

"It's all right," Tristan said to her in a low voice. "No one is looking this way. The airfield guards are keeping their focus tighter around the ships, and the guards here are still compensating for their reduced numbers. The only ones who could even see us are the two in that far tower, and they're not looking this way much."

"Still, I feel like we keep walking right into traps," Lafayette said. "Worse, I'm not sure how we stop doing that."

"We have to get to Uche," Tristan said. "Even if

it is a trap. I can't leave him behind, and I don't think you can either."

Lafayette just shook her head, not trusting herself to speak.

They watched the twelve prisoners who were currently outside as they walked in slow, ambling circles around the far end of the yard. There were only two guards on the ground with them, but if any of the prisoners thought this reduction in security made for an opportunity for escape, they didn't show it. They mostly had their eyes on their own feet as they shuffled along in the slipper-like shoes that had faded from the whitish-gray that the new ones Tristan and Lafayette wore were to the color of the yard dust that coated them.

Uche stood out from the others in more ways than the fact that he wasn't wearing his hat. He followed the same circular path as the others, but he wasn't in single file. He had another prisoner walking right beside him.

This man looked nearly as old as Uche himself, to judge by the deep wrinkles that furrowed his sun-damaged face. But this man, old as he was, appeared to be in peak physical condition. He moved easily without the stooped shuffle of the others. And when Uche stumbled, which he did on several occasions, that man was always there to catch his arm and keep him on his feet. Then he would lean closer to Uche's face, clearly checking that Uche was okay to carry on walking.

He was very deferential. There was a familiarity there, both in how he spoke to Uche and in how Uche answered him. Lafayette couldn't catch their words, but she could read their body language. She was sure the two of them were close. Like old friends. But Uche had only been on the island for, at most, a couple of weeks.

Someone blew a whistle, and the circle of prisoners broke formation. But they didn't change their shuffling pace at all. They just redirected towards the now-open door into the main prison building.

"We have to get his attention," Tristan said. Uche and his companion had been the farthest out when the whistle blew, and Lafayette could see the other man holding Uche's arm, encouraging him to wait for the others to get out of the way before heading to the door themselves. Perhaps to avoid the jostling and crowding at the door itself. Although with only ten other prisoners plus two guards, it was hardly more than a momentary problem.

The other man was still speaking to Uche when Uche, nodding, almost looked towards where Lafayette and Tristan stood in the shadows. He dropped his eyes again, but not before Tristan started waving at him. Uche didn't glance back up again, he just hung his head tiredly as he listened to the man beside him.

But that motion had been enough to draw his companion's attention. His head snapped over to them, the quick response of a hunter on high alert. Tristan stopped waving and retracted his hand, but it was too late. That man was staring right at him and Lafayette both with cold, steely gray eyes.

"Uh-oh," Tristan said as the man said something short to Uche. And then started crossing the yard straight over to where the two of them stood in the shady alcove.

"I hope he's friendly," Lafayette said, just resisting the urge to back up against the door behind her. There was no retreating now. And if they were going to make a run for it, the access corridor behind her wouldn't be where she would start any kind of chase.

It wasn't until the man and Uche had joined them in the late afternoon shadows and no longer had the sun in their eyes that Uche finally looked up at the two of them. Lafayette watched as worry became puzzlement became actual recognition on Uche's face. Then he broke away from the other man's grasp and rushed forward to clasp both Lafayette's and Tristan's hands.

"What are you doing here?" he asked in a rush.

"That's a long story," Lafayette said with a wary glance toward the other man.

"Oh, forgive my manners," Uche said. "Lafayette Eloi, Tristan Carey, this is my very old friend and the first student I mentored, Odilon Rommel."

"Student?" Tristan repeated, looking at the man who had pushed back his hat to give them both a nod. What hair that was left on that man's scalp was sparse and silvery white.

"That was a lifetime ago," Odilon said. "When Uche was a young man himself. He had just became a professor a year before."

"I was so young then," Uche chuckled. "Odilon is also a historian by training, although a bureaucrat by vocation. I haven't seen him since he disappeared nearly fifteen years ago. That was not long after your own parents had to flee the capital, Lafayette."

Lafayette bit her lip but said nothing. But Uche's eyes were on his old friend's face, and there was real fondness there. "I thought for sure I'd never see him again. But then they brought me here, and who came to my aid on my first confusing day here but Odilon Rommel." He gave his head a little shake, like trying to clear it of too many reminiscences. "Well! Now my first student meets my last."

"Surely not the very last," Tristan said, flushing at the unexpected attention.

"But what are you both doing here? And dressed as prisoners?" Uche pressed. "You aren't prisoners here. I would know if they had brought in any more."

"They've been culling our numbers," Odilon said with a frown. "Not adding new ones."

"It's just a kind of camouflage," Tristan said. "We've been hiding here for a few days, but we're about to escape now. And you have to come with us."

"Escape?" Uche said with a frown.

"That's our airship over there," Lafayette said, pointing with her chin.

"The one with the two burly guards standing directly in front of it?" Odilon asked mildly.

"We're working on a plan," Tristan said. "But first we have to get you out of here." Then he swallowed hard before saying, "Margo Weiss is here. For us, I think, but—"

"You think she'll use me to get to you?" Uche interrupted him to say.

"You know she will," Odilon said to him in a low voice. "Uche, this is your chance. You have to take it."

"Oh, no—" Uche started to object.

"Listen, kids," Odilon said, talking over his old mentor. "You have to get him out of here."

"That's our plan," Tristan said.

But Lafayette said, "Why?"

Tristan shot her a look as if he thought she was going crazy, but she kept her own gaze on Odilon.

"Uche still knows things he hasn't told them," Odilon said grimly. "And they know he still knows things he hasn't told them. Uche told me about this Margo Weiss person, and I can gather from what he said that she's surely working for the Secret Investigations branch of Central Planning."

"That's what the red uniform means?" Tristan asked.

"Exactly," Odilon said. "But most SI officers don't wear uniforms at all. For each red uniform you see, you can guarantee there are twenty more Secret Investigations officers around you just blending in."

"So, the guards?" Tristan asked.

"Or even the other prisoners," Odilon said. "You need to get him out of here. Now. What he knows, it needs to stay secret. And it won't. Not if this place is about to be overrun with SI."

"You should come with us, old friend," Uche said, but Odilon was already shaking his head.

"No, go with the kids. I'll cover for you. I've been here longer than anybody, and the guards trust me. I can play for time, especially in all this confusion. I don't think they'll know you're really missing until tomorrow morning at breakfast. I'll make sure they assume you're still around here someplace. I'll buy you all the time I can. But you have to go now."

"Help is on the way," Tristan said to both of them. "We are escaping now, but we can always come back later when we have more of an advantage. Even if your friend has to stay behind now, you'll see each other again. And sooner than fifteen years this time."

"We'll make sure of it," Lafayette added.

Odilon looked back over his shoulder at the two guards still standing in the yard, conferring with each other. Either they had noticed that their headcount was off, or they were concerned about whatever was happening on the other side of the prison. Lafayette was willing to bet it was the latter, given how little information they had had access to while standing out in the yard, too far to chat with the guards in the towers.

But that would likely change in about two seconds. They were already starting to step back from each other.

"I'm going," Odilon said, pushing the three of

them deeper into the shadows before backing away from them. "I'll cover for you. But you need to run. And don't worry about me, Uche. You know I'm tougher than I look."

Uche just nodded, too overcome to speak.

But Lafayette heard Tristan mumble something about how that didn't even seem possible, and she didn't chuckle out loud. Although she did agree. How would it be possible for Odilon to be tougher than he looked? He looked like he could wrestle both of those armed guards to the ground, then sprint up and over the prison walls to escape himself.

"Lafayette," Uche said. "Where is Kora?"

"She's with Dieter," Lafayette said. "We'll all be together soon."

The sun was just starting to kiss the horizon off to the west, past the airfield and the waiting airships. She had been in the tropics long enough now to know that full darkness wasn't far away.

But even as the shadows they were standing in deepened, she still felt so very exposed.

CHAPTER 19

Tristan had taken Uche's arm and was moving him closer to the door, although Lafayette didn't want to go back inside. That felt too trapped, which was worse than feeling too exposed. Or at least she thought so.

But before she could say anything, she heard several people shouting and then the pops of gunfire. She ducked and covered her head, driven by some instinct she couldn't even name. But the shouts and gunfire both were from the other end of the prison compound. Not even the airfield. She thought, from the mental map she had gained from her time up in the tower overrun by birds, that it was coming from the harbor.

But then a shadow passed over them as something moved between where they stood and the setting sun. She spun to see an airship circling out over the water, moving away from the harbor then turning back to head more directly their way.

Tristan and Uche stayed close to the wall, but Lafayette ran further out to the center of the prison exercise yard. The guards who had been on the ground had gone into the building with Odilon, and the guards up in the towers were too distracted by the approaching airship to notice Lafayette.

Or, rather, approaching *airships*. Because two more had drawn up to either side of the first. All the guards were firing at the balloons now, but if any of them were scoring any hits, it wasn't enough to deter those balloons.

Out in the middle of the yard, as far as she could get from the walls of the buildings, Lafayette had a decent enough view of what was going on around her. She saw one of the flanking airships peel off from the others to move over the rooftops, gliding over the prison itself to the tower that had been abandoned to the birds.

And she saw Dieter and Kora up there now. Dieter was standing on the parapet, reaching out to catch the approaching rope ladder that was hanging down from the airship gondola. And Kora was already hovering behind him, with a lead running from her robotic core to a cord tied around Dieter's waist, ready to be towed after him.

Lafayette didn't know if they saw her, or if any of the airship pilots were looking her way. But just in case, she took off her hat and threw it away, fluffing out her hair puffs to full spherical deployment. The red of her hair would have to be her beacon. In the growing darkness of the rapidly falling twilight, she had no other.

Then the second flanking airship moved out of formation, hovering closer to the airfield. It immediately started drawing the bulk of the fire from the guards, leaving the original lead airship mostly unmolested as it continued gliding out over the island.

Directly towards Lafayette.

"Tristan!" Lafayette called, but he was already heading her way. Uche was running beside him with an agility that hadn't been apparent just minutes before when he'd been stumbling around the yard with the other prisoners. Either he had been faking that infirmity, or adrenaline and the hope of rescue were working wonders on his physical state now.

The airship cleared the fence between the airfield and the exercise yard and glided easily over the strange storage structure. It didn't come down any lower over the exercise yard, but the rope ladder that unfurled from the open door of its gondola was more than long enough to reach the ground, its ends dragging through the dry dust.

It would be a long climb up, especially for Uche. But they were so nearly home free.

Lafayette heard a crash and spun to see the door to the prison bursting open. A phalanx of prison guards spilled out, followed by twice their number dressed in Central Planning naval uniforms.

And then came a single, brighter uniform. Margo Weiss in her distinctive volcanic red outfit, strolled nonchalantly out onto the exercise yard.

Lafayette turned away from her to look towards the approaching airship with its dragging rope ladder. It was nearly within her grasp. Then she shifted her attention to Tristan and Uche running towards her. The guards were catching up behind them, but not quickly enough to stop them.

Lafayette caught the ladder, then held it steady, waiting for the other two to reach her first.

Tristan's face was flushed, and he was clearly putting everything he had into sprinting over the packed dirt. But when their eyes met, he still managed to send a grin her way.

But before she could return it, Uche at Tristan's

side tripped. One of his slipper-shoes had slid off his foot, turning his toes so that his step came down more on his ankle than the ball of his foot. Tristan tried to catch him, but there wasn't enough time. Uche went down so fast he couldn't even stop himself with his own hands. He landed directly on his face in an eruption of blood.

Lafayette surged forward, helping him back to his feet even as she never let go of the ladder. The airship was trying to hold position, and the extra length of the ladder itself gave her a little bit of play. But not a lot. She needed to get them all off the ground, and she didn't have much time to do it in.

Tristan got Uche back on his feet, and Uche, mindless of the spurts of blood gushing from what looked like a badly broken nose, staggered forward to catch the ladder. Lafayette held the bottom steady as he scampered up it with more speed than Lafayette would've thought he had left in him.

She gave him half a length of head start, then turned to motion Tristan to follow his mentor.

And he tried to do it. He was ready. But it was too late. The guards were on top of him now. He lunged for the ladder, but two heavy bodies crashed down on top of him.

"Tristan!" Lafayette cried, torn between the

overwhelming desire to run to his aid and the desperate fear that if she let go of that ladder even for an instant that all hope would be lost.

She was basically frozen in place, but Tristan was still moving. Even as more guards joined the pile, he squirmed out from underneath them and, under cover of the growing dark and the even more quickly growing cloud of kicked-up dirt, managed to get back on his feet and continue his run for the ladder.

But Lafayette felt that ladder pulling in her grasp. She hooked an arm through the ropes, but that did nothing to stop the fact that the entire thing was rising up into the air. The airship was ascending almost directly straight up. And it was taking her with it.

"Tristan!" Lafayette called, twisting so that her arm was looped through the ladder, but her other hand was down as low as she could get it. She stretched, reaching out for him even as he ran the last few steps to where she had just been standing.

His fingers brushed against hers, and she seized his wrist in a firm grasp. She wasn't letting go of him. Not this time.

She heard the cracking sound before she'd quite figured out what it meant. Then there was a confusing explosion of pain that started at her wrist but quickly raced all the way up her arm.

She nearly lost her hold on the ladder with her other arm as her whole body reeled in shock.

But she totally lost her hold on Tristan.

One of the guards had hit her with his riot stick, right on the protruding bone of her wrist. It was hard to tell with all the blood and the nonspecific waves of pain, but she thought it might be broken.

She tucked it up against her stomach in some instinctive wound response, then forced her eyes to open and look down.

Tristan was still down there, gazing up at her. Watching her sail away from him, ever higher.

The look on his face was downright blissful. Like he was just content to see that she had made it to freedom.

Then the guards were piling on top of him again, wrestling him back to the ground. From the motion of their arms, Lafayette could tell they were punching him. And they were hitting him with their riot sticks. They were beating him, and were going to keep beating him until he stopped moving. And then they'd probably keep beating him some more.

Something whizzed past Lafayette's ear with a hot whine. The guards were shooting at her now. But with her broken hand, she didn't know how she was going to manage climbing the rest of the ladder. It was all she could do just to hold on.

But before she had gone quite high enough for the darkness to fall between her and the scuffle below, she saw Margo advancing to where Tristan lay under the pile of guards. She had her head tipped back and was looking straight up at La-fayette.

And the grin on her face was one of pure triumph.

The last thing Lafayette saw was Margo commanding the guards to break it up.

Lafayette was sure they would follow orders. But by the time they started to break up their pile, she was both too high up and too far east to see if Tristan was still moving. She twisted as best she could on the end of the ladder, desperately trying to see back down into the exercise yard. But the airship was past the outer walls of the prison now. She no longer had line of sight.

Lafayette hung there for what felt like forever. She sobbed for Tristan, then she sobbed for the pain in her broken wrist. Then she sobbed for Tristan again, because he was surely hurt far more severely than she was.

Eventually, long after the point where the altitude and the evening air had sunk coldly into her bones, she heard someone calling her name. It was mostly drowned out by the wind, but the syllables were clear enough.

She fumbled to get a leg through the bottom rung of the rope ladder. Then she leaned back to look up towards the gondola overhead.

Dieter's fourteen-year-old sister, Finley, was hanging out of the doorway, shouting down to her. Lafayette would know that ragged, gender-less haircut anywhere. But once Finley saw that she had gotten Lafayette's attention, she disappeared back inside the gondola.

And the ladder started to rise. She was being hauled in, but in a series of jerks that definitely would've sent her spilling down into the ocean far below if Finley hadn't warned her it was coming.

Lafayette certainly hoped there was someone stronger than Finley and Uche up there. Because she didn't have the strength left to attempt a one-armed climb herself. And the growing cold was sapping what little strength she had left. Just holding on was becoming a struggle to maintain.

When the ladder finally reached the lip of the gondola doorway, she did have to move to get herself inside. With her wounded hand tucked in her armpit, she reached for the doorway with the other and pulled with all her might to haul herself inside. Someone she couldn't see off to her left reached out, caught the back of her pants, and hefted her into the gondola's interior.

It wasn't the most dignified way to board a vessel. And Lafayette hissed as she landed hard on her broken hand.

But then Uche was there, wrapping a blanket around her shoulders. His nose was taped up, a bright white X of bandages between two fresh black eyes.

"Are you okay?" Lafayette asked him.

"I'm meant to be asking you that," he said. He sounded like he had the worst of all possible head colds, but beyond that his words held good cheer.

"Tristan," she said. Well, she choked it out.

"I know," Uche said, patting her knee. "He's with Odilon. He'll be okay. And the kids here tell me they're going back for the others soon."

"Soon?" Lafayette said.

"As soon as they can," he said with a sorrowful smile. "Now, answer my question. Are you okay? We expected you would climb up here under your own power, but you didn't."

"I think that guard broke my wrist," Lafayette said, pulling her arm out from the folds of the blanket. It was a bloody mess, and it hurt to move, but she didn't really know how bad it was.

"We can set it for you if it's broken," Finley said.

Lafayette looked up at those words. Finley was standing over her with a first aid kit, her brother Archer beside her. Lafayette couldn't remember which of them was older. They had looked interchangeable when last she'd seen them, but that had been when they were both deeply in their street urchin guises.

Now they looked like very short naval officers in the sorts of leathers and long, flowing scarves that Stewart and his crew had been wearing under their parkas. Airship crew uniforms, but not quite the sort Central Planning used. It didn't really work with the urchin haircut they were both sporting, but Lafayette judged another week or two would be enough to grow the last of the shaggy layers out.

"You pulled me inside?" Lafayette asked, and Archer laughed.

"I helped," he said. Then he grinned at her, a grin so very like his brother's in its dry amusement at the world. "I helped by manning the controls. My brothers, Karlo and Till, pulled you in. But they're back in the cockpit now. You'll have to thank them later."

"Is your whole family out here?" Lafayette asked as Finley sat cross-legged in front of her on the gondola floor and gently started washing blood away from Lafayette's wound.

"Not the *whole* family," Archer said.

"Just all the siblings," Finley said as she tossed the dirty square of gauze aside and grabbed a clean square to carry on with her work.

"And some of the cousins," Archer said.

"But not our parents," Finley said.

"Where are your parents?" Lafayette asked.

Uche chuckled, but Lafayette didn't know why until Finley finally said, "They have a revolution to get started first."

CHAPTER 20

The airship Lafayette was on now was a lot like the first one she'd ever seen. She tried to remember how impressive it had seemed the first time she set eyes on it. But the trouble was, she knew how much better the Central Planning airships were.

Not that she cared about comfort or even what food was stocked on board. No, all that mattered now were speed, maneuverability, and range. And the Central Planning airships had the Bohm family airships beat on every single score.

But the Bohm family had a few advantages over Central Planning. The siblings were all skilled pilots, risk-takers when necessary, and very quick with changing their tactics due to changing conditions.

The darkness of night helped, but mostly it was that daring and ingenuity that let Karlo and Till finally shake off the last of their pursuers. Without a cloud in the sky, the moonlight reflected brightly off the sides of the Central Planning balloons. But the Bohm family balloons, being older and more thoroughly patched up in a random assortment of materials, didn't have the same glow.

More importantly, the Bohm siblings had spent the last few days charting every island in the vicinity of the prison island. And they used that knowledge to good advantage now, hiding behind mountains and flying so low over tropical forests that Lafayette was sure she could lean out of the gondola door and touch the fronds of the tallest trees.

Then they'd skip with all due speed to the next rocky outcropping of island while the Central Planning airships were still searching for where they had gone.

But it did take the entire night to get far enough away that they weren't spotted again when the Central Planning ships fanned out in a wider search pattern. When the sky to the east started to lighten, there was no sign of pursuit.

But there was also no sign of the other Bohm family airships.

"Are we the only ones to make it clear?" Lafayette asked as she stood behind Karlo and Till in the cockpit. They were Dieter's oldest siblings, not twins but inclined to dress and keep their hair exactly alike. They were no longer dressed as young professionals working in the capital, but in flying leathers and long red silk scarves. Like Finley and Archer, they looked like they were dressed to put on an entertainment about airship bandits or something.

Not that she would say so out loud. They clearly took their clothing choices very seriously.

"I'm sure we all made it," Till said to her. "The plan was to separate during the escape, and everything seems to have gone according to plan."

"Seems?" Lafayette repeated skeptically.

"We picked you up, just like we were assigned to," he told her. "Ivka got Dieter and your dog on her airship just fine. And Nicolo and Mila jumped from Ronja's airship and succeeded in commandeering your stolen airship."

Lafayette had met Dieter's sisters Ivka and Ronja one time, when they had helped Dieter get the three of them get up into the air with that first airship what felt like a lifetime ago. Those two really were twins, although Ronja's long pink hair and Ivka's shorter, spikier blue did make them easy to tell apart.

Nicolo and Mila she both had never met nor never even heard of. But that was scarcely surprising, considering that Dieter was one of ten Bohm siblings.

Perhaps wondering about her silence, Till turned to look more directly at her. "I'm sorry. Of course, everything didn't go exactly according to plan. We failed to rescue young Tristan Carey. Apologies."

"Uche says his friend Odilon Rommel will look out for him," Lafayette said. "I can just hope that's enough until we can go back for him."

Till looked like he had some thoughts about that, but in the end just gave her a dismissive nod, then turned back to his piloting tasks.

Lafayette wandered to the back of the gondola, where Uche was preparing yet another batch of coffee for them all. He mixed it with so much sugar that the spoon could practically stand up in it, but that was fine. Lafayette didn't mind the sweetness, and the quick jolt of energy from the sugar blended nicely with the longer jolt from the caffeine.

"Finley tells me we're heading to a cavern inside a volcanic caldera," he said to her as he handed her one of the steaming mugs. "Can you imagine? I never thought I'd see such sights as I've seen in the last few weeks."

"I'm sorry about your books," Lafayette blurted out. He blinked at her in surprise, but she kept on. "They burned them all. Margo and her other secret investigations officers. They burned everything from your house, and everything that Tristan was hiding in the secret loft over the library, and everything of my father's I had brought with me. All of it, gone."

"It *is* a shame," he agreed. "But Finley tells me you've been committing everything you remember back to the page. That's good."

"It's all on the other airship," Lafayette said. She wanted to believe that Dieter's siblings had truly succeeded in stealing it back again, but she couldn't quite make herself do it. Not until she saw it for herself. Not until she actually held all of her journals as well as Tristan's in her hands again.

"You'll have it back soon," Uche assured her. "But more than that, Margo didn't find everything."

"Is this what Odilon meant before? That you didn't tell them everything?"

"That's right," Uche said. "He knows another stash exists, and so does Central Planning. But only I know where it is. And no one else would ever be able to find it. Not without me leading them there."

"Books?" Lafayette asked.

"Printed books, but also electronic things scavenged from our ancestors' ships and the remains of their first villages," Uche said.

"Anything like a communicator?" Lafayette asked a little too eagerly.

"Perhaps," Uche said. "But most of it isn't in working order. They are more along the lines of historical artifacts."

"I don't know, I think Dieter can fix just about anything," Lafayette said.

Uche smiled and nodded, then carried the tray laden with coffee mugs first to where Finley and Archer were dozing near the gondola door, then aft to the brothers in the cockpit.

"We'll be there soon," Finley told Lafayette. "You can probably see the mountain from here if you look to the north."

Lafayette took her mug to stand at the right-hand window. The sun wasn't quite over the horizon behind her, but the sky was fading from deep blue to indigo, and the stars were winking out one by one.

And she could indeed see the outline of a single mountain on the northern horizon. The sides were steep, but the top was almost perfectly horizontal. A volcano that had blown its top in some distant time in the past.

Even as she looked at it, the brothers in the cockpit changed their heading from due west to start a slow, lazy circle back around to that island in the north.

She was just about to turn away when a glint of light caught her eye. The first rays of the dawning sun were reflecting off of something very near to that island. Something flying over its beaches.

"That will be Ronja," Finley said, suddenly at Lafayette's elbow. "We aren't using the radios, you know. But I'm sure that's her. She's always the first one back."

Lafayette just nodded, suddenly nervous. They would be landing soon after Ronja, and somewhere out there the other two airships were either already in the cavern or were very close by.

That meant she'd be seeing Kora again soon, and Kora would finally have access to the food she desperately needed.

But it also meant she'd see Dieter again. And she dreaded that moment. She didn't want to have to tell him she had left Tristan behind. She had failed to rescue his best friend.

But worse than that, she feared he would see

her broken wrist and not be angry with her because he was pitying her or something.

She would rather he were angry with her. So she wasn't alone in being angry with herself.

Karlo and Till flew them up higher until they were at the altitude of the top of the caldera. Then they glided gently over the island, even as the sun rose high enough in the sky to set everything in a rosy-gold glow of light.

They made a smaller turn within the caldera itself, just high enough in the sky for Lafayette to see out of the ring of volcanic rock. She saw a glint of an approaching airship to the south, and another further east. Both were heading straight to the island.

Then they were descending to the caldera bottom far below. The volcano had clearly been dormant for a long time, its interior as filled with trees and growing life as the crater to the south of the capital where Lafayette had seen her first spaceship.

There was a jerk as the airship came to a stop, its mooring lines made fast by hands Lafayette couldn't see on the ground below. Then Finley was flinging open the door, and she and Archer leapt out, running to greet whoever waited outside.

"Ready?" Uche asked Lafayette, taking the

empty mug from her hands and setting it aside for her.

Lafayette nodded mutely, then followed him to the gondola door. People Lafayette didn't know—but who were, by their facial structure and clothing choices, clearly either Bohm siblings or Bohm cousins—reached out hands to help first her and then Uche down from the gondola.

It felt like everyone around her was talking at once, greeting one another and trading stories in loud, fast voices. It was all too overwhelming.

Then Till jumped down out of the gondola behind her. He saw her standing apart from the others and smiled at her, then came up to take her by the arm.

"We're meeting down in the cavern," he told her. "I'll show you both the way. There will be food waiting, if I know my aunts."

Lafayette nodded and followed him across the grassy meadow where four airships were already moored, and posts stood waiting for the others to arrive. The grass was sharp and coarse and clearly resisting any effort to trample it down. Its thick greenery also hid a large number of tree stumps cut down close to the sandy ground. This airfield had been hard-earned, and Lafayette could tell it took a lot of work to maintain.

"You were already here when Dieter sent my message out," she guessed.

"Indeed," was all that Till said.

They reached the edge of the meadow where a worn footpath wound through trees and ferns the size of shrubs to the rocky wall of the caldera itself. There was a narrow chasm in that wall that was at first like a canyon open to the sky above, but then took a downward turn into a cave proper. Torches were set just close enough to keep any part of the passage from falling into total darkness.

But the cavern beyond was filled with light from several large bonfires as well as electric lanterns sitting on tables and crates. Till led Lafayette and Uche to the largest of the tables, one so long it had a dozen lanterns set on it and could easily seat at least three times that number.

"I smell pan bread," Uche said, and Lafayette's stomach growled at the words even before she smelled the buttery smell of it herself.

"Fill up," Till said, picking up a large serving platter stacked high with already cooked rounds of pan bread. "There's also fruit in that bowl over there, just a sampling of some of the things we've found on the island. The meeting will start when everyone's arrived."

Lafayette settled onto the bench at the very

end of the table and filled up a plate with pan bread and diced fruit in an array of bright colors. She didn't know what any of it was, but it was all cool and sweet.

But she just chewed it mechanically and wondered what Tristan was eating right now. That terrible applesauce? Something worse? Or possibly nothing at all?

She hated that it depended on Margo's mood. But whatever Margo did to Tristan, Lafayette swore she'd do the same to Margo when their roles were reversed.

Tenfold.

CHAPTER 21

Lafayette heard Kora's barks echoing through the cave entrance and pushed away from the table at once to run to her. It was a strange and alarming sound, Kora barking. Lafayette couldn't remember the last time she had heard it.

But Kora wasn't in any danger. She was just anxious to find Lafayette among the crowds of Bohm family members. Lafayette dropped to her knees as the dog charged into the cavern.

"Lafayette!" Kora said over and over again as she licked all over Lafayette's face. She was jumping up and down the entire time, which meant jostling Lafayette's broken wrist more than once. But it took the third sharp hiss of breath for her to notice. "Lafayette! You're hurt!"

"Just a little break," Lafayette said. "Finley already set it for me. Just try not to bang against the cast."

She hadn't even noticed Dieter there behind Kora, not until he pushed the dog aside to drop to his knees in front of Lafayette. He gingerly took her arm and examined the cast. He gently twisted her arm this way and that before finally letting it go with a grudging grunt of approval.

"She's been working with my aunt, then," he said. Then he looked up into Lafayette's eyes. "How does it feel?"

Lafayette blinked back tears. "Tristan—"

"They told me about Tristan," he said dismissively. Then leaned in to look at her even more intensely. "How does it feel?"

"If I don't move it around too much, I don't really notice it," Lafayette said. Which was almost true. But mostly because the throbbing ache of it had faded into part of the general background noise of worry and sorrow in her mind.

"I'm going to have my aunt look it over. Not that I doubt Finley's work or anything. Just, my aunt will have a better idea of how long it will take to heal," Dieter said. Then he stood back up and started looking around the room. "It'll have to wait. They're gathering at the table. Let me help you up."

Lafayette nodded and extended her good arm. He hoisted her up to her feet, then led her with Kora trailing close behind back to where Uche was still sitting at the table.

"Good to see you, boy," Uche said to Dieter with real warmth in his tone.

"Sorry we couldn't make it to you sooner, sir," Dieter said. "My family was already planning to break you out of that prison. Once they knew you were here and not in the capital, they came down in full force. But they were still in the planning stages when they got my—or rather Lafayette's—message."

"They're still planning it," Lafayette told him. "Finley said so. They came in to get us, but they're still intending to free everyone."

"Yes," Dieter said, but distractedly.

"Including Tristan," Lafayette said.

Dieter looked up at her at that and reached across the table to squeeze her good hand. "You got hurt trying to save him. You did all you could, but we were very outnumbered. No one blames you for what happened, least of all me."

Lafayette nodded mutely.

"My former student Odilon Rommel will look out for him," Uche said.

"Odilon Rommel?" said Karlo from further down the table. "Why does that name sound familiar?"

"He was one of the last graduating class with a history major, back before Central Planning started dictating the history curriculum and transforming it into the propaganda machine it is today," Uche said.

"I don't read much history," Karlo said musingly.

"He didn't pursue it as a career, alas," Uche said. "I mentored him for as long as I could, but he grew too frustrated by the restrictions. Every year, more restrictions on what we could study, what we could read for research, what we could teach or say. He left it behind in favor of a low-level bureaucrat job. But that was nearly fifty years ago."

"Bureaucrat? You mean he works in Central Planning?" Dieter asked.

"He did," Uche corrected. "As many did and still do. But he never gave up on his search for more knowledge. He had a secret library in the basement of his house. He was hoarding as many of the banned books as he could. It was a sizable library, but it was all destroyed fifteen years ago."

"About the same time as my parents left the capital," Lafayette put in.

"Those were chaotic times," Uche said. "A lot of

students were reporting each other as well as teachers and librarians for studying unapproved histories, or preserving copies in hiding after Central Planning goons went through all our shelves at the university, purging anything they didn't agree with."

"And Odilon Rommel was arrested when his own books were destroyed?" Dieter asked.

"Yes. And he's been on that island ever since. Fifteen years," Uche said with a shake of his head. "I can't imagine it. Of course, when he first got there, it was packed with people. There was a lot of disease and never enough food."

Lafayette tuned out Dieter's words of comfort and support, distracted by her memory of Odilon Rommel. He had been very fit for a man of his age. He was almost impossibly fit for a man who had spent fifteen years in such dismal conditions. Even if it were marginally better now, how had he recovered so completely?

"Odilon Rommel!" Karlo suddenly exclaimed, slapping his hands down on the table. "I know where I heard that name. He was part of the early days of the failed rebellion. Dad knew him."

"Oh, right," Ronja said from across the table, nodding as her own memories returned. "Yeah, Dad said the rebellion didn't really fail until this Rommel fellow disappeared. I don't know if Dad ever knew he was arrested for book hoarding, though."

"He must've known," Karlo said. "But when we get back to the capital, we can ask him more about it."

"You're going back to the capital?" Dieter asked in alarm. "I thought we were taking the island."

"We're doing that too," Karlo said, with a nod towards his sister Ronja. Her mouth was full of pan bread, but she lifted her hand in the air.

"Won't we need all ships to take the island?" Dieter asked.

"We're splitting up to lure the ships away," Karlo said. "Till and I are going back to the capital in our airship."

"The slowest in the Bohm fleet," Till said. "We'll be going slow enough to pick up some tails, but not slow enough to get caught. Like a mother bird pretending to be wounded to lure predators away from her chicks."

"Okay," Dieter said, then looked to Ronja.

"Ivka is going to pretend she's heading north, back the way you were going when you left us," Ronja said. "You found something up in the north, didn't you?"

"We did," Dieter said.

"It's all gone now," Lafayette added. "They

sank it to the bottom of the ocean under a glacier of ice."

"Doesn't matter," Ivka said with a shake of her head. "All they have to think is that *I* think I can get to it. Or get to something worth their effort of stopping me from achieving my goal."

"Which is to lure off more ships," Dieter guessed.

"Right," Ivka said.

"And once that's done, I'll fly in on my airship," Ronja said. "It has the most carrying capacity for passengers. So I can bring a ground force in large enough to overthrow the remaining guards on the island, and then start ferrying the prisoners here to safety."

"They'll find this place," Dieter said.

"Eventually," Ronja said, but with a grin and a tilt of her head. As if she relished the thought.

"What about us?" Lafayette asked.

"Nicolo and Mila are stocking up your airship now," Till told them. "You'll be ready to be underway by nightfall."

"And where are we going?" Lafayette asked. "Because I want to be part of that ground force taking the prison, if it's all the same to the rest of you."

"Well," Till said, looking pointedly at her wrist.

"This will heal," she said, raising her chin.

"My team is accustomed to working together," Ronja said. "Together, but not with strangers. Sorry, I think our odds of success are much higher if we don't start throwing random elements in."

Lafayette felt her cheeks heat at being dismissed as a random element. But before she could muster any words, Uche's voice spoke up.

"I should very much like to get back to the capital," he said, looking to Karlo and Till. "Is there going to be room on your airship?"

"Of course, Professor Okafo," Karlo said.

"Your stash?" Lafayette asked. "The books and things?"

"Yes, I think it's time to unearth them all," Uche said to her. "They just might make the difference between the first failed rebellion and whatever we have going on now."

"I should go with you, then," Lafayette said.

But Karlo was already shaking his head, "No. That wouldn't be a good idea."

"Surely by the time an airship can get to the capital, I'll be healed up," Lafayette said.

"It's not that," Karlo said.

"You and Uche are both high-value targets in the eyes of Central Planning," Till told her. "We've intercepted a lot of their encrypted messages, and we know that they already have you on the highest security list, along with Professor Okafo."

"We can't risk having you both in the same place," Till said. "Even having you both here until nightfall is a big risk."

"I will be all right on my own, Lafayette," Uche said, putting a hand on her arm. "And I know you will be too. And we'll meet again someday. Possibly a day that's sooner than we think."

"But what am I going to do?" Lafayette asked. "I can't just sit here waiting."

"Oh, no. That's not the plan at all," Dieter said. Then he gave her a grin, albeit one that didn't quite reach his eyes. Still, she knew he was trying for lighthearted when he said, "You and I have a mission of our own."

It was only then that Lafayette realized that Dieter's name hadn't come up yet in the breakdown of what all the airships were doing.

"We're both going with Nicolo and Mila?" Lafayette asked.

"Indeed," Dieter said.

"But where?" she asked.

"The only place that makes sense," Dieter said. "We still have one more ship to find."

"You mean the ship that went down in the mountains to the south?" Lafayette asked. "The ship that didn't appear on the systemic field with the rest of the fleet when we were using the communications console on the ship under the ice?"

"It might be unique among the ships of the fleet in that it crashed more than landed," Dieter said. "It's entirely possible there is simply nothing left."

"But heading south will draw off another measure of ships, particularly the airships," Nicolo said.

But Dieter waved that away as if it were of lesser importance. Although drawing off the ships was what was going to help get Tristan free.

"What are you hoping we'll find?" Lafayette asked.

"Maybe nothing," Dieter admitted with a shrug. "But maybe something. Just because the communications console on board that ship was no longer connected to the systemic field doesn't mean that it's gone. It could just be switched off."

"But we've never seen anything switched off before," Lafayette said. "We've only found everything running on minimal life support. Even the ship my father found was technically on before he started touching things. Otherwise nothing would've happened, right?"

"There might be nothing there," Dieter said again. "But, you know, there just might be. And how will we know for sure if we don't go look for it?"

Lafayette chewed at her lip. She wanted to be

more excited about this prospect. Uche was safe now, but there was still her father she had to find a way to save. This mission might help with that.

Or it might just be a huge waste of time.

But something else struck her, and she stared right into Dieter's eyes. "You're not as recognizable as I am. In fact, you're a bit of a chameleon."

Dieter shrugged and tried not to look too impressed with himself.

But Lafayette went on. "You don't have to go south to the mountains just to avoid danger. You could storm the prison island or even go back to the capital if you wanted."

"I could," he allowed. "But I won't. Do you really think I've come all this way not to see this through?"

"But Tristan—" Lafayette started to say.

"Would want me to stay with you," Dieter said firmly. "And that's exactly what I'm going to do."

"The mountains to the south are high," Lafayette said. "I think maybe even too high for airships."

"We have gear for trekking," Dieter said. "I have a feeling we're going to have to do a lot of that to find what we're looking for. Because if it were obvious, Central Planning would have it in their hands already."

"All those messages," Lafayette said. "From all

across space. I really wish we'd gotten a chance to play them back. To hear their voices even if we couldn't understand their words."

"We'll get the chance again," Dieter said. "But first, we have one last ship to find."

"One last ship," Lafayette said.

She had been on the top of the world. She had been under ice and deep underwater. She'd been as far west, north, and east as anyone on her planet had ever been. It kind of felt right, to go to the south. To the highest elevation it was possible to climb to.

She wished Tristan were there with her. Of course she did.

But she had Dieter. And he had her. And they both had Kora.

They could do this.

"Right," Lafayette said. "Let's go find the last ship."

She would get those messages from across space, and she would find a way to tell everyone in the world just what they all said. Despite what Central Planning wanted them to believe, they weren't alone in the universe.

She was going to find a way to tell them all that truth.

CHECK OUT BOOK FIVE

History sleeps beneath them all, and she will wield it.

Lafayette Eloi started her journey as an ordinary girl from an inconsequential village deep in the grasslands of her home world. But that start lies so far in her past now. And she has endured so much loss since then. Her mother dead, her father trapped in a derelict ship out of her reach in orbit around her world.

Her close friend Tristan Carey now in the hands of the government that hunts her still, desperate to cover up all the secrets that Lafayette knows.

But for Lafayette and Tristan's best friend Dieter Bohm, any desperate attempt at a rescue mission must wait. A fifth ship, another wealth of secrets, waits for them to the south. The government wants to race her there, to destroy this ship as they destroyed the others. Lafayette can't let that happen.

Because inside that ship lies the key to rescuing her father. And, just maybe, freeing every person under the oppressive rule of her world's government. All she has to do is get there first.

Ransacking the Taken Past, Book 5 of **The Forgotten Planet** YA sci-fi series, available November 10, 2026 direct from me or December 8, 2026 in stores everywhere.

SCI-FI SERIAL PODCAST!

Check out my new monthly podcast of serialized science fiction: THE TALES OF THE CHAI MAKHANI TRIO!

Elyot loathes the massive Commonwealth ships that hover menacingly over his home world of Adghal. He hates the Commonwealth enforcers who harass the populace even more. But with his mother missing and presumed dead, Elyot keeps his head down and strives to avoid notice. And he succeeds until the day two strangers enter his life...

New episodes of this sci-fi serial drop every 1st of the month.

Now streaming on Apple Podcasts, Google Podcasts, Spotify, Stitcher and more. Also available in eBook and print everywhere books or sold. For a complete episode listing, check out the page on my website.

COMPLETE SERIES: THE TRAVELS OF SCOUT SHANNON

The complete six-book series THE TRAVELS OF SCOUT SHANNON begin with book one, Under Falling Skies.

Scout Shannon's whole family died the day the Space Farers dropped an asteroid on their domed city. Now she lives alone, out in the wild with only her dogs for company. She prefers it that way.

But Scout finds herself at a crossroads. One road leads back to a quiet life snug under the protective dome of a city. The other road leads to a life in the rebellion, a life of adventure and excitement but also danger. Dare she try to find the rebels hiding in the hills?

Then a chance encounter with a stranger from the other side of the galaxy threatens to derail what remains of Scout's life. The entire galaxy awaits her, if she survives the next four days.

"Under Falling Skies", a young adult science fiction novel, set on a remote planet with a distinctly Old West feel. For fans of gunslinging women and young girl assassins. And dogs.

Under Falling Skies, the first book in THE TRAVELS OF SCOUT SHANNON, available everywhere now.

COMPLETE SERIES: THE RITCHIE AND FITZ SCI-FI MURDER MYSTERIES

The Ritchie and Fitz Sci-Fi Murder Mysteries starts with Murder on the Intergalactic Railway.

For Murdina Ritchie, acceptance at the Oymyakon Foreign Service Academy means one last chance at her dream of becoming a diplomat for the Union of Free Worlds. For Shackleton Fitz IV, it represents his last chance not to fail out of military service entirely.

Strange that fate should throw them together now, among the last group of students admitted after the start of the semester. They had once shared the strongest of friendships. But that all ended a long time ago.

But when an insufferable but politically important woman turns up murdered, the two agree to put their differences aside and work together to solve the case.

Because the murderer might strike again. But more importantly, solving a murder would just have to impress the dour colonel who clearly thinks neither of them belong at his academy.

Murder on the Intergalactic Railway, the first book in the Ritchie and Fitz Sci-Fi Murder Mysteries.

ALSO FROM KATE MACLEOD

Love heists and capers? Then check out my new series, THE VIC HARPER CAPERS. The action starts with the novella THE THIRD POLE JOB.

Vic Harper and her gang retired wealthy from their life of thievery and heists. Whether in a luxury condo overlooking the river in Minneapolis or in a modernist mansion built into the side of a mountain in Colorado, life comes easy now.

Perhaps too easy.

When an old friend asks for a favor his niece, Vic and her mentor Chase Woodward leap at the chance to relieve a little of the boredom. But a quick bit of B&E in a wealthy suburb of Chicago leads to an even greater challenge.

The prize? Nothing much. Just the opportunity to level a playing field for their friend's niece.

But the heist? May prove to be their toughest ever. Because to get to the prize, they'll have to climb a mountain.

And not just any mountain. Their prize waits on the summit of Mount Everest.

THE THIRD POLE JOB, the first novella in the Vic Harper Caper series. For those who love capers, heists and other impossible missions.

ALSO FROM RATATOSKR PRESS

Also from Ratatoskr Press, The Witches Three Cozy Mystery Series by Cate Martin, a mix of mystery and magic that begins with Book 1: Charm School.

Amanda Clarke thinks of herself as perfectly ordinary in every way. Just a small-town girl who serves breakfast all day in a little diner nestled next to the highway, nothing but dairy farms for miles around. She fits in there.

But then an old woman she never met dies, and Amanda was named in her will. Now Amanda packs a bag and heads to the big city, to Miss Zenobia Weekes' Charm School for Exceptional Young Ladies. And it's not in just any neighborhood. No, she finds herself on Summit

Avenue in St. Paul, a street lined with gorgeous old houses, the former homes of lumber barons, railroad millionaires, even the writer F. Scott Fitzgerald. Why, Amanda can practically hear the jazz music still playing across the decades.

Scratch that. The music really, literally, still plays in the backyard of the charm school. Because the house stretches across time itself. Without a witch to protect this tear in the fabric of the world, anything can spill over. Like music.

Or like murder.

The complete series is out now, and it all starts with Charm School.

FREE EBOOK!

Like exclusive, free content?

To get two prequel short stories to THE RITCHIE AND FITZ SCI-FI MURDER MYSTERIES as well as a bonus prequel novelette to the completed six-book series THE TRAVELS OF SCOUT SHANNON, signup for my monthly newsletter at KateMacLeodWrites.com.

Thank you!

ABOUT THE AUTHOR

Kate MacLeod has written stories which have appeared in Analog, Strange Horizons and Mythic Delirium, among other places. She is also the author of two young adult science fictions series: The Travels of Scout Shannon, and The Ritchie and Fitz Sci-Fi Murder Mysteries. She also contributes to a serialized science fiction podcast called The Tales of the Chai Makhani Trio. She currently lives in Minneapolis, Minnesota.

Find out more about the author and sign up for her newsletter at KateMacLeodWrites.com.

ALSO BY KATE MACLEOD

Novels

The Slums of the Solar System:

Mitwa

The Mars of Malcontents

The Whole World for Each

Books 1-3 Box Set

The Travels of Scout Shannon:

Under Falling Skies

In Quaking Hills

Among Treacherous Stars

Against Impassable Barriers

Over Freezing Altitudes

At Galactic Central

The Travels of Scout Shannon Books 1-3

The Travels of Scout Shannon Books 4-6

The Travels of Scout Shannon Books 1-6

The Ritchie and Fitz Sci-Fi Murder Mysteries:

Murder on the Intergalactic Railway

Murder in the Skies

Body in the Catacombs

Death on the Summit

An Undiplomatic Murder

A Lethal Betrayal

The Ritchie and Fitz Sci-Fi Murder Mysteries Books 1-3

The Ritchie and Fitz Sci-Fi Murder Mysteries Books 4-6

The Forgotten Planet

Raiding the Forgotten Derelict

Plundering the Planetary Secrets

Salvaging the Arctic Wreck

Foraging the Hidden Sanctuary

Ransacking the Taken Past (Available November 10, 2026 direct from me or December 8, 2026 in stores everywhere)

Sci-Fi Novellas

The Intergenerational Tree

I Rise into a Daybreak

Caper Novellas

The Third Pole Job

The Twelve Days of Christmas Job

10-Story Collections

Tales of Blood and Ink

Tales of Old Gods and New

Tales of Spaceships and Magic

5-Story Collections

Tales from Heian-Kyo and Others

Tales from the Edges and Ends

Tales from Forgotten Days

Tales from Ancient and Future Times

Tales From Across Space

Tales from Places Strange and Familiar